D1055451

John Creasey

Writing as Jeremy York

Murder in the Family

David McKay Company, Inc.
Ives Washburn, Inc.
New York

First American Edition, 1976

Library of Congress Catalog Card Number: 76-1554
ISBN: 0-679-50609-8

MANUFACTURED IN THE UNITED STATES OF AMERICA

Contents

Murder in the Family

Chapter 1

The Apple Blossom

Valerie Fayne turned from the drive gates and ran to the house, followed by a cocker spaniel eager to join in any excitement. Rushing through the hall and up the stairs ahead of her, he led the way to the landing. The window was wide open and the curtains were billowing outwards; downstairs, a door slammed in the wind.

The spaniel whined in excitement, and looked up at her inquiringly. She put a hand down to smooth his head.

'You're quite right, Jinx,' she said. 'I *am* a fool!'

She leaned out of the window straining her eyes to see beyond the beech trees which screened the road running straight over the brow of the hill.

She fancied that she could hear the hum of Robin's car as it came into sight, rushing with surprising speed away from her.

'Good-bye, Robin!' she called. 'Until Friday!'

The car reached the top of the hill, then it disappeared, leaving the road deserted. She stood there for some seconds, as if hoping her husband would come back, then turned away, giving Jinx an absent minded pat.

He stood looking up at her.

'Jinx,' she said slowly, 'I could sit down and *cry*! It's crazy isn't it? He'll be back early on Friday evening, and it's Tuesday now. Only three days, and yet – '

Jinx whined hopefully, but apparently gathered from her expression that high spirits no longer prevailed. He began to walk about the landing restlessly. Valerie went back into the bedroom and pulled the clothes back from the large four-poster bed which was unmade. Mixed up with them, was Robin's pyjama jacket.

She hugged it to her, then laughed, and folded it neatly as a good wife should.

'This just won't do!' she chided herself. 'He'll be away

a great deal, and I'll have to get used to it.' Rather at a loss, she looked out of the window again. It was a perfect morning for spending in the garden, neither too hot nor too cold; she would do that.

Going downstairs, she met the postman, whom she already knew by sight. She had discovered that Felshire people were friendly with strangers, and the postman was no exception. He had only one letter, which he held in a browned hand, while his wizened face wrinkled in a smile.

'*Beaut*iful marnin', it be.' His voice was gentle and slow. 'Glass be going up,' he added. 'I must be getting along. Good-morning, ma'am.'

'Good-morning,' said Valerie. 'Thank you.' She held the letter loosely, as she watched him mount his bicycle and ride away. The postmark, she noticed, was London, but it was neither that nor the bold, familiar hand-writing of her sister which made her smile, it was the name, *Mrs* Robin Fayne.

The *Mrs* fascinated her.

Ten days before, she had been Valerie Marshall; and only four days before, marrying Robin in the registrar's office in Chelsea, she had seen The Paddocks for the first time – this old Tudor house, charming at a first glance and growing more attractive to her every day. Much still seemed new and strange, but as she walked through the house to the back door, opening the letter as she went, she was conscious of a deep pride in The Paddocks. She had lost her earlier fears that it would be impossible to run so large a house unaided, for Robin had performed a miracle, and conjured up a woman from the village who would come in every day.

Jinx was padding along just in front of her. The letter – a brief, excited note from Julie – was in the pocket of her smock.

Mrs North, the elderly help, stout, and voluble, arrived just as a clock in the hall struck nine. It was ten minutes before Valerie, feeling slightly guilty, escaped from the house.

The previous tenant of The Paddocks had taken his gardener with him, but had left the grounds in perfect order. Valerie strolled along a grass path, with neat rows of young green shoots coming up on either side.

Dividing the kitchen garden from the small orchard, was a row of beech trees. If Valerie had a regret, it was that the beeches, now in full leaf, hid the orchard from the house. From where she was, she could see some of the fruit trees, their blossom varying from the white of the flower to the deep pink of the buds. There were fifty-eight trees in all – one for each of their combined years, Robin had said laughingly; he was thirty-three, and she was twenty-five.

The trees on the right of the orchard were laden with twice the weight of blossom as the others. There were eight of them! All Bramley's. When they had strolled about the orchard the previous evening, those eight trees had looked as if they were covered with pink snow. Hardly a leaf or a twig had been visible. Unable to resist the temptation to look at them again, Valerie pressed on. The grass in the orchard, in need of scything, was wet with dew, for it had been a mild winter followed by warm spring rain and many hours of sunshine. Enchanted by the beauty of the scene, Valerie, for the first time, forgot that Robin would not be back for three days.

Then she saw the eight trees – and stopped.

Nothing else had changed, the air was full of light and movement, but Valerie's smile faded, her expression of happiness changed to one of shock and incredulity.

There was no blossom on the Bramley's!

They were shorn of their promise, and the grass beneath them covered with a carpet of petals. It was as if a giant hand had struck them down. In a daze, Valerie picked up a twig, which was heavily-laden with flowers not yet faded.

'I – I can't believe it!' she said, unsteadily. 'I just can't believe it!'

The spray she was holding had been cut through with a knife, and the end was damp with sap. Dazedly, she inspected the blossoms about her and found that not all been cut; some had been shaken or pulled off.

Slowly it dawned on her that it had been done deliberately. It was not a question of an accident, or the careless vandalism of thoughtless play; and there had been no frost or wind.

Valerie pushed her hair back from her forehead, and shivered; yet it was not cold even out of the sun. Bewilderedly, she turned back to the house.

A clatter of crockery told her that Mrs North was washing up. She did not feel like talking to anyone but Robin, and bitterly regretted his early departure. With luck, she hoped, she could get through the kitchen without being delayed. But Mrs North, rubbing vigorously at a brown tea-pot, glanced up with a wide smile. It faded quickly.

'Lack-a-day!' she exclaimed, 'whatever be the matter?'

'M-matter?' stammered Valerie.

'Why, look at yourself, Mis' Fayne, you're as white as a sheet! Just look at yourself!' She stood gaping. 'Have you had bad news?' continued Mrs North in a hushed voice, putting the tea-pot down and drawing nearer.

'N-no,' said Valerie. 'That is – I mean – oh, I can't understand it!' In a flash her attitude changed, colour came back to her cheeks, and her eyes sparkled. 'It's an incredible thing, a beastly act of – of utter destructiveness!'

'W-what is?' Mrs North insisted, with pleasurable excitement. 'What is, Mis' Fayne?'

'The orchard!' stormed Valerie. 'Some brute has been in during the night and cut all the blossom off the best trees!' Leaving Mrs North standing staring after her, she hurried to the telephone.

'Give me the police, please,' she said sharply.

After a lengthy delay, due, not so much to lack of interest on the post-mistress's part as to a country attitude towards time, a pleasant, broad-vowelled voice said:

'Pelshire Constabulary. Who is speaking?'

'It's Mrs Fayne,' said Valerie, beginning to wonder how to broach the subject; to tell a policeman that the blossom had gone from some apple trees might strike him as being utterly unworthy of his attention.

'Mrs *Who?* asked the policeman.

'Mrs Fayne, of –'

'Oh, I mind ye,' said the man quickly. 'Mrs Fayne of The Paddocks. Good-marnin', ma'am. Can I help ye?'

'I – I don't quite know,' admitted Valerie. 'Someone has been damaging my orchard. It isn't just a prank,' she added quickly. 'It – it's – well, it's *spiteful*. Will you come and see me as soon as you can?'

'Why, yes, ma'm,' said the constable, promptly enough to make her feel a little easier. 'Don't move anything, if you please.'

He rang off before she could speak again. She put back the receiver, and then stared out of the little window, from which she could see one of the three large paddocks – now ploughed and sown with wheat – after which the house had been named. Small green shoots were breaking through the earth, tender and beautiful.

'I must pull myself together,' said Valerie, aloud.

Mrs North, returning from a visit to the orchard, was muttering angrily to herself. By the clash of china, Valerie deduced that the shock necessitated a further pot of tea.

Presently she heard footsteps on the gravel drive, and from the window, she saw the heavily-built village policeman Tom Carrow, walking beside a tall, thin man, who was dressed in dark clothes and was wearing a clerical collar.

'The parson!' thought Valerie. 'Now, of all times!'

She felt exasperated that he should call at so inopportune a moment, yet when she reached the hall, and found him standing in the porch, she found it impossible to be annoyed with anyone so friendly.

'Mrs Fayne?' He did not wait for her to say 'yes'. 'I was passing Tom's cottage as he came out, and when I heard what had happened, I thought I would come along with him. I do hope you don't mind.'

'It was nice of you to think of coming,' said Valerie. 'Please come in.'

'I'd like to go straight to the scene of the offence, ma'am,' broke in P.C. Carrow stolidly. 'You can't act too quick over a thing like this, that's my opinion. It isn't as if it were the first – '

He broke off, because the Rev. John Frend glanced at him sharply; but he had said enough for Valerie to be able to finish the sentence for herself adding the one word 'time'.

She said quickly: 'What do you mean? Has something like this happened before?'

In the momentary pause before either of them answered, she knew that it had.

Chapter 2

Not The First Offence

Carrow's bright blue eyes flickered for a moment, then he cleared his throat.

'It has, ma'am, I won't be denying it. Two or three places in the village have been affected – '

'You mean – other orchards – '

'Not orchards alone,' declared Carrow. He made a harassed movement towards the door. 'I'd like to see it, ma'am, without delay.'

'Come this way,' said Valerie, 'it's quicker.'

As she walked between Carrow and Frend towards the orchard, she was remembering, with a touch of uneasiness, Carrow's hesitation. She glanced covertly at the vicar, who was looking straight ahead of him, unsmilingly. His profile was sharp and impressive.

Jinx bounded enthusiastically ahead of them, while Mrs North watched grimly from the kitchen window.

As they neared the gap between the trees, Carrow lengthened his stride, peering about him purposefully. The heavily laden trees made it impossible to see as far as the Bramleys, and he turned to Valerie.

'This way,' she said, taking the lead.

She ducked beneath a sweeping branch, and as she emerged she saw a man standing by the nearest tree regarding the scene blankly. So unexpected was his presence that she gave a startled exclamation.

The man turned and looked at her. He was old and small and grey. Gravely he lifted a hat as weathered as himself.

'Marnin', ma'am. I – '

From behind Valerie stalked P.C. Carrow. The stranger's gaze, though motionless, became hostile. Carrow's voice, throaty, intimate, and yet official, cut through the silence

'I *thought* so! I want a word with *you*, Battley.'

Battley turned away deliberately and looked at the vicar.

'Marnin', Vicar.'

'Good-morning Amos,' said Frend, pleasantly. 'This is a sorry business, isn't it?'

'Aye,' agreed Battley, turning to survey the mass of fallen blossom.

'Where were *you* last night?' Carrow demanded, in a voice laden with suspicion.

'In bed – where you ought to have been,' said Battley.

'Whoever was responsible certainly made a job of it,' said Frend, with a smile of professional conciliation. 'I am really sorry, Mrs Fayne. It is such a miserable welcome to Pelham!'

'It seems so senseless,' said Valerie, waiting for a constructive suggestion from Carrow who, obviously labouring under considerable emotion not unconnected with Amos Battley, now seemed unlikely to give one.

It was Battley who broke a long silence.

'Can I help you clear it up, ma'am?'

'You'll leave it be!' snapped Carrow, his words coming out like pistol shots. 'Understand this, you'll leave it be! The sergeant will want to see about this. Nothing more I can do for now, ma'am, 'cept send a man to watch the garden for you meanwhiles.'

Without expression, Battley touched his hat to Valerie and the vicar and moved away. Carrow stared after him, hostility written all over his florid countenance.

Valerie wondered who the old man was and why Carrow should be so antagonistic to him. She was annoyed with the policeman, for if Battley were prepared to clear the blossom, he might be persuaded to accept regular work.

'Isn't it a bit pointless to have the orchard watched in daylight?' she asked.

'You never know,' said Carrow, cryptically. 'You'll excuse me, ma'am. Marnin' Vicar.' He touched his forehead and then strode off in the wake of Amos Battley.

Valerie pressed her hand against her forehead; her head was aching dully and she felt bewildered and out of her depth. She thought Carrow's decision absurd. Soon the 'sergeant' would be visiting her, and he would probably adopt an attitude similar to Carrow's

'You must feel rather confused,' said Frend, as they began to walk towards the house.

'All acts of wanton vandalism are rather frightening.'

'But you're not alone are you?' asked Frend anxiously.

'Unfortunately my husband is away for a few days.' Valerie led the way to the side door. 'You'll come in, won't you?'

They went through the main hall into the low-ceilinged sitting-room. Frend lowered his head automatically as he passed beneath the oak beams, as if he were used to the room. She suggested tea or coffee, but he refused, saying he had not long had breakfast. He sat in an easy chair, stretching his long legs, his hands resting on the wooden arms.

Valerie asked abruptly:

'Was Carrow telling the truth?'

She half-expected Frend to hedge, but he smiled faintly.

'Not altogether, Mrs Fayne. This is not, in fact, the first time there has been trouble at The Paddocks.'

'Oh!' said Valerie. She sat down heavily. 'When the other tenants were here, do you mean?'

'Yes.' Frend put his hand to his coat pocket, and Valerie could see the outline of a pipe, touched lingeringly.

He was easily persuaded to light up. Everything he did appeared to be the calm deliberation of a man who never hurried. Obviously he knew something which was distasteful to him and which he did not want to discuss, but felt that he should. The room was very quiet, and Valerie began to wish that he would break his long silence; his hesitancy was disquieting.

'Ye-es,' he said, at last, 'the previous tenant, Mr Dering, was very proud of his garden – he is an enthusiast, as you may know, his own gardener travels with him wherever he goes. He had some very rare orchids in the small hot-house. One day in the winter, the windows were removed and the heating system damaged. The frost killed many of his most treasured plants. It upset him very much indeed. There were one or two other things – some of his crops were stolen last year, and damage was done to others. Similar happenings occurred at other large houses in the district, but – ' Frend paused, then asked: 'You'd like to hear about all this, wouldn't you?'

'Please,' said Valerie.

'The general opinion, which Tom Carrow shares, is that Amos Battley is responsible for anything that goes wrong at The Paddocks. Before the Derings' came here, Battley had worked in the garden all his life. And a very good job he did – Dering's gardener could not have done better. I felt very sorry for Amos when he was paid off, and there's no doubt that he took it badly. The garden was part of his life, in fact, his only interest.'

'You don't agree with the general opinion?' said Valerie.

Frend shook his head. 'I find it difficult to believe that a man would try to ruin something which he had built up himself. Since Amos left, two years ago, he's looked after the little patch at his cottage, and refused to take work elsewhere. He's over seventy, but there's no better gardener in Pelshire! Did you notice how quickly he asked permission to clear up the blossom for you?'

'Ye-es,' said Valerie, slowly. 'I wished Carrow hadn't said "no". Do you think –' she broke off.

Frend laughed.

'Yes, I do think Battley would come and work for you, if you were to approach him,' he said. 'And I think that we would probably find that the other trouble would continue, so that suspicions of Amos would die a natural death.'

'I'll see him this morning,' said Valerie, decisively.

'Good!' Frend's eyes held approval. 'It will make a new man of him.'

'But if he didn't damage my fruit trees, who did?' asked Valerie. 'And why? Battley has got a reason of sorts, although he has nothing against Robin and me. I can't understand why anyone else should try to damage the garden.'

'No,' admitted Frend, gravely, 'that's just the problem.'

'Look here!' said Valerie, bluntly. 'Do you know anything else?'

'Nothing at all,' Frend assured her. 'I am as bewildered and shocked as you are at the thought that anyone nearby would deliberately rob or damage gardens. I've grown very fond of Pelham in the seven years that I have been here.' He turned adroitly from the subject. 'I should have called before to welcome you. I hope you will forgive me. The people here are a pleasant, self-contained little community, and I am sure you will like them.'

'I was sure too,' said Valerie, with a troubled smile, 'until this extraordinary affair in the orchard!'

'Don't let it affect you too much,' advised Frend. 'Now – as you're alone today, why don't you come and have tea at the Vicarage? My sister would very much like to meet you.'

'Thank you, I will come,' said Valerie, impulsively.

'Good! Helen will tell you how lucky you are to have The Paddocks – we all love the house, you know. In the Mottrams' time – they were Amos Battley's employers, and lived here for fifty years – the garden was a show-place. You didn't know the house then, did you?'

'I didn't, but my husband did,' said Valerie.

She found herself talking freely, telling him that Robin's mother had been a Mottram, and that The Paddocks was as renowned in his family as it was in Pelham. An elderly uncle of Robin's had owned the house, and had leased it to Robin – she omitted to say that the uncle did not allow sentiment to interfere with business and that the rent was pretty stiff.

It seemed to Valerie that Frend already knew all that she was telling him. He left her with a vague feeling of disquiet, which lingered long after he had gone.

He had told her that Amos Battley lived in a small cottage on the outskirts of the village, and she decided she would visit the three local shops, and walk on to see the old man. She felt that P.C. Carrow would not approve, but this conviction only added a grim satisfaction to her resolve.

Before reaching Battley's cottage, she passed a small picturesque garage, before which an old man was tinkering with a bicycle. Seized with a sudden idea, Valerie walked over to him.

He looked up with a slow, friendly smile.

'I was just wondering if there's any chance of you having a bicycle for sale,' said Valerie, 'in fact, two – one for myself and one for my husband?'

'Ar,' said the man with his head on one side. 'Now you've set me a problem, ma'am. A leddy's bike, now, that I could supply. Second-hand, mind ye, but as good as new when I've finished with 'un. I couldn't do it less'n five pounds,' he added speculatively.

'Oh, that would be all right.'

'If ye were to wait a matter of ten minutes, ye can take it with ye. This be it.' He waved to the bicycle on which he had been fitting new brakes, a sturdy roadster strapped with a carrier and a basket.

'I'll be passing this way in about twenty minutes,' said Valerie. 'May I collect it then? I'm living at The Paddocks.'

'Ah,' said the old man with no show of surprise, squinting professionally at the handle-bars. 'I'm Joe Parker, ma'am, an' I get to know most folks pretty soon after they come.'

'I'd like to have the basket on the bicycle as well, if I may.'

'Oh, ah! It's all in the price,' said Parker. 'I don't hold wi' making profit on little bits and pieces. Now as for the gentleman's bike, shall I keep my eye open for 'un?'

'Please do,' said Valerie, 'I'd be very glad.'

But for the trouble at the orchard, and the vague misgivings with which Frend had filled her, she would have been thoroughly happy. Parker's manner, indicative of the friendliness of the village people, augured well for the future. She was humming a little to herself when she reached a bend in the road. Beyond it, on the right, was the church of St Mary, and, not a hundred yards further along, was Amos Battley's cottage.

As she drew near, she heard a familiar voice raised.

'Ye'll come with me, and no arguin', Battley. Do ye want me to use *force*?'

'That's Carrow!' thought Valerie. She was angry and alarmed as she realised that the policeman was arresting the old man.

The front door was open and the voices travelled clearly, Carrow's loud and blustering, and Battley's calm and contemptuous. With admirable restraint, the gardener was telling Carrow what he thought of him, and as Valerie reached the window Carrow shouted:

'Stop your talk, you old fool! And come wi' me!'

He put a hand on Battley's arm.

On seeing Valerie, Carrow pulled up short; Battley, although he looked surprised, came forward and touched his forehead, saying:

'Can I help ye, ma'am?'

Valerie decided to pretend that she had heard nothing of the conversation. She forced a smile, ignoring Carrow.

'I think you can, Mr Battley. I need help in the garden at The Paddocks, and I wondered if –'

'At The *Paddocks*!' breathed Battley.

The vicar had said that a job at the house would infuse new life into Battley; and now Valerie knew that it was literally true. For the first time Battley smiled. He took a short step forward, and his whole body seemed to grow more erect.

'At The Paddocks!' he repeated. 'Aye, that I will, ma'am! I –'

He stopped abruptly.

The light died out of his eyes and his shoulders sagged.

'He won't be working for *any*one for a time,' said Carrow, roughly, 'and I don't think *you'll* want to employ him, ma'am – not after you've seen – this!'

He bent down, and picked something up from the floor. Valerie was astounded to see the small flowering branch of an apple tree.

Helplessly, she looked at Battley, whose deep-set brown eyes did not falter.

'I brought 'un away early this marnin', ma'am. I came back, ma'am, when you found me, to tell you what had happened. That's all I know.' He looked contemptuously at Carrow. 'I hope when this bother is settled, ma'am, I may have the pleasure of working for you.'

Under the disapproving eye of Carrow, Valerie said evenly:

'My offer still stands, of course, and I hope it won't be long before you can come.'

'Thank ye, ma'am,' said Battley.

There was no point in staying longer, and Valerie walked thoughtfully back to the garage. She was not surprised to learn that Joe Parker had been over-optimistic in reckoning the time taken on repairs. He promised to deliver the machine however, that afternoon, and Valerie hurried on her way.

She had finished her lunch, and it was nearly half-past one, when there was a ring at the front door. She went to open it herself. A man stood in the porch, his face vaguely familiar.

He introduced himself brusquely, as Inspector Webb of the Pelshire Police, and asked if he might have a few words with her.

'I suppose it's about the orchard?' Valerie inquired, leading the way into the sitting-room, surprised that the incident should be thought worthy of an Inspector's attention.

'Yes, it is,' said Webb, crisply. He looked intelligent, though not outstandingly so, and Valerie hoped for a less biased attitude than shown by Carrow. 'The damage to your garden is one of a series of offences, Mrs Fayne. That is why I am attending to it personally. I have inspected the damage

– it was, of course, quite deliberately done.'

'I told your constable that,' said Valerie sharply, deciding with disappointed resentment that she liked Webb little better than Carrow.

'So I understand,' said Webb. He smiled faintly, 'I also understand that you have offered to employ Battley?'

'I have,' said Valerie, coldly.

'Did you have any particular reason for that?' asked Webb.

'Yes.' Valerie drew a deep breath. 'A *most* particular reason, Inspector. I want the garden tended.'

'I see. You had no other reason?'

'No, but I don't see the need for these questions.'

'I'm afraid I often have to ask questions which seem unnecessary,' said Webb. 'You've heard Battley's account of how he came by the sprig of blossom?'

'Yes. It seems quite a natural one,' said Valerie.

'I am inclined to agree,' admitted Webb, 'although the village constable does not! I've questioned Battley, and he sticks to his story. If it were anyone but he, I would think it unlikely, but his affection for the house is quite a by-word. So I have released him, for the time being, pending further inquiry.'

'How sensible of you!' exclaimed Valerie.

He looked at her sharply.

'There is just one other thing. As you doubtless know, from the field at the end of the orchard there is an excellent view of the village. The moon will be rising about dusk, tonight, and I want to station a man in a position where he can see most of the village gardens, and thus be able to notice any night prowlers. Have you any objection to a man being stationed in the field?'

Valerie hesitated.

There was nothing against it, and she doubted whether anything she said could prevent the police doing what they liked. It was something deeper which made her hesitate – a feeling that it was The Paddocks he wanted watched rather than the village.

She said slowly:

'Are you really so interested in the village, Inspector? Or are you more concerned with The Paddocks?'

As soon as she had spoken the words she wished that she

could withdraw them. Webb's smile faded, and he looked at her narrowly.

'Why should you think that I am particularly interested in this house, Mrs Fayne? Have you any reason for thinking that I am?'

Valerie hesitated, not knowing quite what to say, conscious of the fact that she was colouring, and that Webb's eyes were filled with suspicion; but she could not imagine why his manner had changed so subtly and to such an extent.

Chapter 3

Mystery by Night

'I have no reason at all,' said Valerie stiffly. 'Except that there was trouble here last night, and it has been suggested that it might be repeated.'

Webb stared at her steadily, for some seconds. Then he shrugged his shoulders and smiled again, but in nothing like as friendly a fashion as before.

'So you have no objection to my man being stationed in the field?'

'None at all,' said Valerie coldly. 'I hope that you will soon find whoever is causing the trouble, so that Battley need not be hounded.'

'Hounded?' echoed Webb. 'A somewhat peculiar word to use, surely?'

'A somewhat peculiar thing to do. No unbiased person hearing Carrow talking to Battley would be likely to doubt it,' said Valerie pleasantly.

She wondered, when Webb had gone, whether she had been right to implicate Carrow – and whether it was not perhaps she who was biased in her natural sympathy for the under-dog.

Battley called soon after. He made no mention of the episode with the police, merely waiting for instructions. Valerie deliberated, Robin could not really afford a full-time gardener – the rent of the house was very high and the running expenses would be heavy. She suggested that Battley should work every other day. He seemed quite happy at the prospect, and agreed without hesitation to wait until Robin's return before arranging terms.

'I don't know a great deal about gardening, so I'm going to leave you to work as you think best,' Valerie said.

Battley's face settled into lines of satisfaction.

'Ma'am, I've worked the soil at The Paddocks so long I

know every grain of it, but I'll be content to do your bidding any time you like.'

Valerie smiled.

'That's splendid!' she said. 'When will you start?'

'Tomorrow,' said Battley,' and I can come on Mondays, We'nsdays and Fridays. Maybe I'll be looking in at odd times on other days, but you won't be minding that?'

'Of course not,' said Valerie.

'Then wi' your permission, I'll take a look at the tools,' said Battley, promptly.

Half-an-hour later, he was hoeing the strawberry beds.

Valerie spent an hour in the morning-room, which they were going to use as a study.

Robin had a voluminous correspondence, to which he was accustomed to attend at week-ends. She was able to type, and had a slight knowledge of shorthand, so she could handle the bulk of the mail for him. Telling him of her decision to do this, she doubted whether he had really taken her seriously; for he had a light and imponderable way of taking life which was part of the charm he had for her. Nevertheless she was determined, and fully confident in her ability to help him, for she had spent four months in the Government Department which he served. It was during this time she had met him, and fallen in love.

Had anyone told her that she would marry a man of whom she knew so little, that she would allow herself to be carried off her feet in a whirlwind courtship of three weeks, she would have smiled in disbelief. Even now, she hardly realised that it had happened.

Her job was both interesting and important, and a replacement for such a position was not easy; but Robin had managed to put through her resignation with smooth efficiency. He seemed to have a natural bent for overcoming difficulties and making the seemingly impossible happen.

She put on a plain linen frock, and presented herself at the vicarage just before four o'clock. She was not surprised by the size of the large Georgian house, for she had known many vicarages; but the quality of the furniture impressed her. A beautifully carved settle faced her in the hall, backed by a tapestry depicting a medieval battle scene, the beauty of which even a subdued light could not wholly hide.

Frend appeared almost at once, leading her into a large, sunny room towards a woman, older than himself, sitting in a wheel chair. Valerie's instantaneous sympathy was shot with surprise, for Frend had said nothing about his sister being an invalid. Yet her pale face, the thinness of her hands, and the grey of her hair, showed that she was, indeed, a sick woman.

She smiled up at Valerie, greeting her in a voice as charming as her brother's. They had tea in the same room, served from a table gleaming with Spode and old silver. Everything about the house, its rare treasures, its occupants, charmed Valerie. Yet she learned little about them.

Frend saw her as far as the gate before he asked about Battley, and seemed pleased when she told him she was employing him.

Home again, she found herself wondering about the couple, and glad that Robin had chosen this particular village. Difficulties and problems no longer worried her, and she relegated the Bramley blossom to the back of her mind.

Just why she went to the attic she did not know. She had not visited it with Robin, and found it large, even spacious, with a low ceiling, hiding the beams and rafters.

Old pieces of furniture, some of them broken, were ranged round the walls. A pile of trunks was near the window, and next to them an easel, bearing a picture. A palette and some brushes were on the floor.

The picture was a portrait in oils, recently restored and varnished. The man's face was vaguely familiar, as someone she knew, but could not place. The discovery made her explore further, and she found several other canvases, some restored, others old and dark, and with the varnish cracked; two had been damaged by damp.

One was of an old man, very like the subject of the first portrait, the second, much more recent was of a man dressed in a modern lounge suit. And he, too, reminded her of someone. She wondered if they were relatives of Robin. The more she thought about it, the more she felt that it was Robin whom they resembled.

To see the portraits better, she took them downstairs to the sitting-room, where the evening light made the face of the man in the contemporary clothes look almost life-like. He was nearly bald, his features small, his lips thin and compressed.

Then Valerie exclaimed aloud:

'I've got it! Robin's uncle!'

She had seen a photograph of Uncle Silas, who owned The Paddocks; now that she remembered it, there was no doubt at all that this was a portrait of him – Uncle Silas, Robin's mother's brother, a bachelor, a solicitor and, if Robin were to be believed, a 'typical Mottram'. By that, he meant tight-fisted.

Glad that she had at last placed the man, she left the portraits in the sitting-room, listened to the nine o'clock news, then admitted reluctantly that despite the excitement of the day, she felt lonely. She was not going to like staying here on her own for long periods, and going to bed too early, she decided that possibly, even probably, she would take a part-time job.

She did not fall asleep quickly.

The longer she lay there, looking towards the window where the moon shone into a corner of the room, the more she thought of the policeman stationed at the other end of the field. She began to brood over the fate of the apple trees. She had not been aware of the night noises when Robin had been with her, but now the walls seemed to creak and whisper. Odd little sounds disturbed the silence. The rustle of a curtain, blown in by a strong gust of wind, made her start and sit up in bed.

She strained her ears, growing increasingly convinced she could hear voices. The longer she listened, the more certain she became. Men were talking in the garden. She pulled a wrap about her shoulders, and went to the window.

As she reached it, she saw a man moving along the path leading to the orchard. Further along, she saw other men. She was not sure, but she thought one of them was Inspector Webb.

Obviously, Webb had wanted to do much more than just station a man in the garden. She felt annoyed that he had adopted such a devious method, and was still angry when, after pulling on a pair of slacks and a thick sweater, she ran quickly downstairs. If Webb had wanted to search the garden, he should have said so. It was intolerable that he should have gone about it so furtively.

She left the silent house almost with relief, and hurried through a gap in the trees. Thrusting onward she gave a sudden, stifled exclamation, for a man came out of the shadows in front of her.

'Good-evening, Mrs Fayne,' said Inspector Webb, calmly.

'I hardly expected you to be up.

'What are you doing in the garden?' cried Valerie heatedly, furious that he might have heard her gasp of fright. 'Is this what you call "stationing a man" in the field?'

'I found it necessary to go a little further than that,' Webb said, his voice even, and unhurried. 'We're clearing the blossom from under the trees, Mrs Fayne – I assure you that we shall not damage anything! What brought you out?'

'You did,' said Valerie. 'I don't approve of you using my garden as if – as if – ' The more she thought about it, the more angry she became. 'I won't allow it!'

'Come – ' said Webb.

'I won't allow it!' repeated Valerie fiercely. 'You've no right to do this without consulting me.'

Webb's voice grew cold.

'I have the right, Mrs Fayne. I have a search-warrant. I thought it would be better if I carried out the work without causing you anxiety, that is all.'

Valerie's anger dissolved into something deeper and more frightening. Webb would not say that he had a search warrant unless it were so – and there was no way of making him explain his reasons. She felt a cold certainty that this official interest did not concern the Bramleys alone.

'I think it would have been much better if you had told me what you proposed to do,' she said at last.

'I am sorry to have caused you alarm,' said Webb, in a tone in which sorrow held no part.

'How long are you going to be Inspector?'

'Not too long, I hope,' he replied, evasively. 'Now I think – '

He broke off, at an exclamation from a man, unseen, working in the orchard. Something had been discovered. Webb half-turned, speaking as he moved.

'I think you would be wise to return to the house,' Mrs Fayne.'

He moved resolutely away to the group of shadowed men, the subdued, excited voices. It was impossible to close her mind to the fact that men were digging. She jumped as a figure materialised at her elbow.

'It be me, ma'am – Amos Battley.'

'I – I don't know what to do,' said Valerie, helplessly.

'Maybe I should go and watch, and tell you what is found,' said Battley.

'Ye-es – no! No, I'll go myself. Battley, ought you to let them see you?'

'I care naught about whether they see me or no,' said Battley, sturdily.

They walked together, making no attempt at concealment, until they drew within sight of the row of Bramleys. All the blossom had been cleared from beneath three trees, and half from a fourth. About the latter, three men were digging.

'Be careful!' Webb cried, warningly. Then he looked at Valerie. 'I see you ignored my advice, Mrs Fayne.'

'This is my garden,' she retorted, in the brave voice of a defiant child.

Webb shrugged, but said nothing more. Battley stood watching, and Valerie felt herself trembling, not altogether because of the crispness of the night air. The men were digging deliberately now, cautiously. Valerie tried to keep silent, but at last the suspense was too much for her.

What are you looking for?' she asked.

'You will see,' said Webb.

The diggers were prodding with a deadly persistence, stolidly and without haste, their breathing heavy and laboured.

Then a man spoke in a sharp voice.

'Here's something, sir!'

'Stop using the spades,' ordered Webb. 'Use the trowels, and don't go too hard.'

The three men went on their knees and began to ply the trowels, tossing little pieces of earth on the growing heap at the side.

Almost against her will, Valerie went nearer.

Chapter 4

The Discovery

It was some time before Valerie realised what the men had found. Oddly enough, when the discovery was made she sighed, almost with relief. She did not yet actually think of it as a body that had once known happiness and grief; even when the men stopped using the trowels and scooped up handfuls of the soft, rich earth, gradually clearing it from the shape which lay, dark and macabre, beneath the shadow of the stripped branches and in the pale light of the moon.

Then she saw the toe-cap of a shoe.

She gasped, and half-turned. Webb looked at her, speaking with a more kindly note in his voice.

'I think you would be wise to go away, Mrs Fayne.'

'I – I'll see it out,' said Valerie doggedly.

Webb nodded, then appeared to lose all interest in her.

The other shoe was uncovered, then the arm and leg of a man. Webb himself went down on his hands and knees and began to clear the soil away from the face. Fighting against a growing nausea, Valerie saw Webb gently raise the dead man's head. The moon shone on pallid features and closed eyes.

At last, Valerie turned away.

She nearly fainted as she reached the beech trees. Battley, half supporting, half leading her, waited patiently, until after a while, he urged her to the house. Reaching the kitchen he closed the door and switched on the light.

'Sit down, ma'am,' he said. He pushed an old Windsor chair towards her, then busied himself with preparing tea.

Valerie took a cup thankfully. 'You – you'll have one, won't you?'

'Thank ye, ma'am,' said Battley.

He stood silently by the stove, drinking his tea and looking at her steadily. When she managed to drive the memory of that pale, lifeless face from her mind, she saw that he was smiling at her, a little grimly.

Surprisingly, he said:

'You'll forgive me speaking out of place, ma'm, but I'm minded of old Mrs Mottram. The *first* Mrs Mottram,' he added, with faint emphasis.

'Do I look like her?' asked Valerie, taken unawares.

'Aye. 'Tis the way she looked when her first-born died of the fever. She couldn't rightly believe it, ma'am. Ten year, I was at the time – doing odd jobs about this kitchen, the way I am now. It's a mighty long time, ma'am. Sixty-four years, come Whit Sunday. Sixty-four years,' he repeated softly. 'Aye, it's a tidy long time!'

'And – you'd worked here all the time until – ' Valerie broke off, at a loss for words.

'Until Mr Dering told me I weren't wanted,' said Battley. 'Little more than two years ago, that be. Aye.' He drained his cup. 'I took it hard, ma'am. I won't deny. I reckoned to live and die working at The Paddocks, long o' the family. Mr Fayne, now, he be Miss Amelia's son.'

So Battley knew that, Valerie thought, startled.

'I saw the likeness,' Battley went on. 'He might be Mr Charles come back to life again.'

'Mr Charles?' echoed Valerie.

'Aye. Fifty years ago I first saw Mr Charles, the very first time he left his mother's room, ma'am. He was killed in the last war. A fine, upstanding man, Mr Charles, the image of your Mr Fayne.' Battley was looking towards her, but she did not think that he saw her; his eyes were half-closed and he was living in the past. 'There was the first Mrs Mottram – her husband died 'fore I came here, but I mind him. As a boy, I mind him walking beside the river, and across the paddocks. A fine judge of a horse, the first Mr Mottram. His pride was the house and estate, ma'am, and his son James was mindful of that. A grand old gentleman, Mr James.'

'Yes?' said Valerie, faintly.

The names were vaguely familiar; Robin had given her a brief resume of his family history, explaining how it was that the house had been left to Uncle Silas, a townsman who took no interest at all in the country, and little in The Paddocks.

'Mr James looked after it well, ma'am. He had a good wife, and five children. Charles, Robert, Silas – Silas was the oldest, ma'am, ye'll mind that. And two daughters, Miss Amelia, and Miss Robina.'

'Robina!' exclaimed Valerie. Robin had told her that he had been named after an aunt, now dead.

'Now there's only Robert's children left, and Miss Amelia's. Four – four in all, and no more,' Battley added sombrely.

'Five,' corrected Valerie, quickly. 'Robin's brother and two cousins – and Uncle Silas.'

'Oh, aye,' said Battley. 'I'd forgotten un.'

She did not really think that he had forgotten Uncle Silas, but he showed no further desire to talk, and she did not press the point.

She was recalling what Robin had said to her about the family. He saw little of his cousins – one was a man some years his senior, the other a girl much younger – and, for that matter, he spoke little of his brother Charles, who was in the Navy. Since the family had thinned out, its few remaining members had lost the old clannishness, according to Robin. At the time, she had thought he had said so with a sigh.

Battley had put the family in a better perspective; she believed she could remember each one clearly, now, right down from the 'first' Mrs Mottram. Then she stopped thinking of the past which was so unfamiliar to her, for she heard footsteps outside the back door.

Someone knocked and Battley glanced at her.

'Yes, open it,' she said. She stood up and looked towards the door.

Webb came in.

With his arrival, she was overcome with a sense of urgency and alarm. A body, a dead man, buried in the garden – *her* garden! In a flash, she realised what it would mean: An investigation, police on the premises, questions, perhaps an inquest. The body of a man in the garden – put there by someone, buried there deliberately!

'I would like to use the telephone, Mrs Fayne,' said Webb.

'Of course,' said Valerie, stepping to the inner door. 'I'll show you the way.' She did not know why she hurried, but Webb kept pace with her while Battley stayed in the kitchen. Webb thanked her gravely when he reached the study, but, before he lifted the telephone, he said:

'Don't go, please!'

He was soon connected with the police station at Listow, the Pelshire County town, twenty-odd miles from Pelham. He gave brief instructions; he wanted photographers and finger-print men, and someone to take casts of footsteps. He wanted the police-surgeon, and – at about eight o'clock the next morning – an ambulance.

Then he rang off and turned towards Valerie.

'I'm sorry to have to cause you so much bother,' he said, 'but I shall have to ask for the use of a room for the rest of the night.'

'Which room? asked Valerie.

'Any one on this floor,' Webb said. 'We shall have to bring the body in here.' He did not make the statement roughly or brutally, but immediately she was filled with a sense of repugnance.

'Why?' she demanded. 'I don't see that it's necessary.'

'I'm afraid you'll have to take my word for it,' said Webb. 'Please don't make it more difficult – believe me, I understand how you feel. I won't make it any worse than I can help, I assure you.'

Valerie was suddenly aware of her solitude, without friends – and without Robin. Friday had seemed a long way off that morning; it seemed twice as far now.

There was something else – a word which she would not allow herself to utter, but which beat relentlessly in her mind. A dead man, a murdered man – *murder*! She felt quite sure of it, and believed that Webb was equally sure. For some reason unknown to her, he had suspected that the body might be in the garden and he had deliberately kept the possibility back from her earlier in the day. She did not know whether to be pleased or sorry about his reticence. Nerveless and inert, she felt herself surrounded by difficulties not of her own making, she could scarcely remember her past happiness and contentment.

'When will you be bringing it – him – in?' she asked.

'Not for an hour, or a little more,' Webb told her. 'We have to photograph the body at the spot where we found it.' His calmness dispelled something of the horror; he made it sound an everyday affair. 'Will this room be convenient?'

'Here? Oh, no, I work in here! There – there's a small room next to the kitchen. Won't that be all right?'

'Anywhere will do,' said Webb. 'Perhaps you'll show me the way?'

He approved the room, which held a small camp bed. Then he went to the kitchen, where a uniformed man reported that Battley had left the house. The fact seemed to strike Webb as being significant. He asked sharply:

'Was he followed?'

'Yes, sir.'

'That's all right,' said Webb, crisply. 'Mrs Fayne, I think you had better go to your room and get some rest. I won't disturb you, I assure you.'

'I'm all right,' said Valerie.

He shrugged his shoulders, as if sloughing all responsibility for her, as he turned and followed the policeman. The door closed with a vibrating echo.

She did not realise until then how much she had relied on Battley's company. The house seemed suddenly strangely eerie and frightening. The friendly kitchen took on a sinister air which made her nervous of the cupboards and corners. The single word 'murder' ran persistently through her mind. Why had a murdered man been buried in the orchard? Why *there*, of all places? Why had Webb suspected that something was beneath the apple-blossom? And why had Battley been followed? Did they think he knew anything about it?

She stayed in the kitchen, too-frightened to move to any other part of the house. The hours passed slowly. Several times, she thought that she heard men approaching, but it always proved to be a false alarm. It was cold, and she wanted a coat; her watch told her that it was half-past two, and she had been up for nearly two hours. As she shivered for a third time in as many minutes, she rose abruptly. She would get the coat.

The switch for the hall light was near the front door and, although she left the kitchen light burning, the corners and beams hid it, so that she had to go most of the way in darkness. An underbreath of sound crept through the house, faint and mocking, and she quickened her pace towards the door. It was a relief when the hall was flooded with light.

Then she thought she saw a moving shadow on the wall by the staircase.

She gasped and stared towards it, her heart standing still. The shadow also remained. Her heart began to beat fast and her breath came quickly, until it dawned on her that the shadow was of a vase, which was standing on a chest on the landing. She forced herself to go forward.

Half-way up the stairs, she heard a muffled and prolonged whine.

'Jinx!' she exclaimed. 'Oh, Jinx!'

She had not seen him since going to bed, and had assumed that he was out, roaming the grounds, for he was by nature a wanderer. Inexpressibly relieved, she hurried up to the landing and turned to her bedroom, from where, she thought, the scraping sound came.

'All right, Jinx!' she called. 'All right, old boy!' She opened the door of the bedroom, but there was no break in the dog's yelping – he must be in the little dressing-room next door. How on earth had he managed to get shut in there? She had not been in the dressing-room that night.

She stopped short.

She had not been in the dressing-room, yet Jinx was shut in there.

Rigidly she opened the door, and Jinx bounded out; but her mind refused to obey, refused to believe, when she told herself reasoningly that she *must* have been in the dressing-room that night. Coldly, soberly, she knew that she had not.

She fought against believing that a stranger had been upstairs, yet her fear grew in intensity. The landing light, bright and unusually clear, spread as far as the middle of the secondary staircase which led to the attic, as well as half-way down the main stairs. It shone along the narrow passage where the spare rooms were, and illuminated part of the hall. Oddly-shaped shadows showed against the panelling of the walls, and the cream wall-paper above the panelling. Except for Jinx, breathing gustily, she could hear nothing.

'Be quiet, Jinx,' she ordered. 'Quiet!' He obeyed, and for a few seconds, there was silence.

'Come with me,' she said, unsteadily.

She rushed to her room, took up a light cloak, and hurried to the landing again. She was in the hall when a sudden shriek of sound tore through the house. Her startled fear, released, flying about her, was flung back by the calming touch of familiarity. Of course. The front door bell.

Her relief was so great that, opening the door, seeing Frend standing there, she stared wordlessly.

Frend stepped inside, then looked at her steadily, with a faint smile at his lips.

'You should have telephoned for me,' he told her, as if admonishing a child.

'How did you know anything was the matter?'

'Battley came and told me,' Frend said. He followed her into the sitting-room, taking his pipe from the pocket of his ill-fitting jacket.

'May I?' His eyes crinkled at the corners. 'Thanks.' Slowly, his long, pale fingers began to fill the bowl.

'How much did Battley tell you?' Valerie asked.

'Pretty well everything, I should think. He's very jealous of The Paddocks, and now that he's back again, he'll guard it with his life! It *has* been a pretty nasty shock, hasn't it?' he added. 'Look here – ' He seemed suddenly much younger, and a little uncertain of himself – 'will you come to the vicarage? In the morning, when you get back, you'll feel rested and more able to cope.'

She was reluctant to say 'Yes', although the suggestion attracted her.

She said nervously: 'I don't want Webb to suspect me of running away. It's silly, I know, but I don't think he trusts me.'

Frend said nothing.

'And I've annoyed him,' went on Valerie, quickly. 'I made it clear that I thought he should have told me what he was going to do.'

'Should he?' Frend seemed to examine the question. 'I think we might accredit him with good motives. It would have been much better if you had known nothing about it till the morning, wouldn't it? And if they had discovered nothing, you need never have known what they expected to find.'

Although he spoke lightly, there was something significant in the word 'expected', and it brought Valerie up with a start.

'Yes,' she said slowly, 'but *why* did they expect to find a body?'

'Hasn't Webb said anything to explain?'

'He seems to take delight in being mysterious,' said Valerie, shortly. 'It must amuse him.'

Frend's eyes narrowed, but he smiled:

'The police have their little ways. Webb –'

Jinx gave a sudden, expectant bark, staring at the door, his tail wagging slowly. In a flash the extraordinary affair of the dressing-room came back to Valerie. Hurriedly she outlined it to Frend who, saying nothing, flung the sitting-room door open.

'This will be Webb, I expect,' he said reassuringly. He statred towards the hall, and as he moved Valerie saw that it was in darkness.

Yet she had left the light on.

'Webb!' called Frend, sharply.

There was no answer, but there was a noise. A swishing sound at first, then an exclamation from Frend. He backed into the room as something moved swiftly and viciously towards his head; it looked like the top of a walking stick, with a crooked handle. Frend fell against the wall and the stick disappeared. The door was pulled to from outside.

It happened so quickly that Valerie could not comprehend it. Before she could speak Frend straightened up and jumped forward. He reached the window in a couple of strides and flung back the curtains; later, she remembered that he seemed to know exactly how they were hung.

'Put the light out!' he called.

Automatically, she obeyed. Frend climbed out of the window, and as her eyes grew accustomed to the moonlight, Valerie saw someone – a man – moving on the drive, about twenty yards away.

Frend jumped to the ground and raced after him. First one, then the other disappeared into the fitful darkness.

Chapter 5

Morning

Although both men were out of sight, their footsteps could be clearly heard, dying away as others from the back of the house, grew louder. Valerie saw two uniformed policemen tearing along in Frend's wake, hesitating at the gates, each going on in an opposite direction.

Jinx, who had jumped out of the window, had given up the chase and was investigating the shrubs on either side of the drive. Valerie watched him affectionately, thinking how useless a part he had played, wishing he were more aggressive with strangers. Then she heard a car approaching, the headlights shining along the drive. It was followed by a second smaller car.

She heard someone in the hall, but the footsteps were firm, no attempt was made to conceal the newcomers' presence. She was not surprised to see Webb, with Battley in close attendance. Webb regarded Valerie inquiringly.

'Who ran away from here?' he asked.

'I don't know,' said Valerie. 'Someone was in the house, upstairs. Mr Frend was with me, and we heard a movement. At least, Jinx did.'

'You've no idea who it was?' Webb insisted.

'*Idea?*' repeated Valerie innocently. 'I thought ideas were anathema to policemen – excepting their own of course. Still you encourage me to say, I had an impression that there was someone upstairs before Mr Frend arrived,' She told him as clearly as she could, what had happened, expecting Webb to tell her that she should have called him at once. Instead, he nodded slowly.

'I see. You're having a most disturbed night, Mrs Fayne, don't you think it would be wise to go somewhere else? I'm sure Mr Frend and his sister would be glad to put a room at your disposal. I don't need to worry you again till the morning.'

It was on the tip of her tongue to ask him why he wanted to worry her at all, but she stopped herself in time. The appeal of a few hours complete rest was almost irresistible, but The Paddocks was her home, and here she was staying.

'I don't think I'm likely to sleep, wherever I am,' she said stubbornly.

'Just as you wish,' said Webb.

The two cars had been driven round to the back of the house, and now Carrow, and a thick-set man carrying a doctor's bag, appeared from the kitchen quarters.

'Mrs Fayne,' said Webb, 'this is Dr Pemberton.'

'How do you do.' Pemberton's gaze was shrewd and disconcertingly direct. 'You look very tired, Mrs Fayne – is there any need for you to stay up?'

He did not wait for her denial or agreement, but continued confidently: 'Take a couple of aspirins and a cup of hot milk, and then tumble into bed. You'll sleep like a top!'

'I'll station a man outside your room,' Webb offered unexpectedly, pleased, Valerie thought shrewdly at this chance of getting rid of her. But she had no intention of letting Webb and Carrow search the house unaccompanied.

Tagging along behind them she saw that nothing appeared to be out of place; her room was just the same as she had left it, and the little dressing-room starkly unaltered. The spare rooms and the music-room remained as desolate and unused as before.

Webb made little comment, beyond asking whether Valerie knew of anything that might have attracted a thief.

She shook her head.

'We'd better have a look in the attic,' he said. 'Are you coming up?'

'Yes,' said Valerie quickly.

His firm and deliberate step ascended the narrow staircase. Soon he called down, and Carrow stepped aside for her to precede him.

As she entered the attic, she thought with surprise that Webb seemed just as familiar with the house as Frend had been. Then all irrelevant thought fled from her mind.

The attic looked as though a tornado had passed through it!

The three large cabin trunks had been emptied and turned on their sides, their contents spread about the floor. Odd pieces of linen, boxes, small ornaments, pieces of china and a hundred-and-one other things, lay strewn in haphazard heaps. The drawers of the several chests were open, the easel overturned, together with half-a-dozen or more canvases.

She looked again, searchingly.

The canvases had been cut out of their frames!

Webb picked up the nearest. The job had been done well; a sharp knife had been drawn down the edges but the frames themselves had not been damaged. Webb cursorily inspected the others, speaking as he did so.

'Were the pictures valuable, Mrs Fayne?'

'I don't know,' said Valerie, helplessly. 'They were portraits, some old, some new. I can't imagine that they were valuable enough to steal, or they wouldn't have been left in the attic.'

'Perhaps not,' said Webb. 'How many were there?'

'I'm not quite sure. About a dozen, perhaps. I took two downstairs, because they seemed to be relatives of my husband. They're in the sitting-room now.'

'Let's make sure of that,' said Webb.

The pictures were just where she had left them. Webb looked at them expressionlessly, and made no comment as he put them back. The animosity which Valerie had felt towards him earlier began to fade. He was being considerate and, perhaps because he was tired, he appeared less official.

'It looks as if we found what our merchant was after,' he said. 'Hello! Someone is coming up the drive. All right, I'll see who it is.' He went out, and a moment later Valerie heard Frend's voice.

The vicar had lost his quarry. The man had completely disappeared, and Frend had returned to report. He would like, he said, to stay at The Paddocks for an hour, if she had no objection. Valerie, going upstairs, knew that Frend was staying because he thought that it might make her feel easier. She felt a deep sense of gratitude at so kindly a gesture.

Answering a tap on her door, she found Battley, with Carrow standing suspiciously in the background. He held a tray with a glass of hot milk and a bottle of aspirins.

'I minded this,' he said, putting it down gently on a bed-side table. 'Good-night, ma'am.'

'Thank you, Battley,' said Valerie, 'You're very good!'

'I'm happy to serve you, ma'am.'

Sitting up in bed, drinking the milk, it occurred to her that she ought to telephone Robin. After a few mintues consideration she decided to put through a call early in the morning. Soon, she began to feel drowsy, and she went to sleep.

She slept heavily, troubled by dreams of stolen canvases.

She was awakened the next morning by a motor-vehicle turning in front of the house. By the throb of its engine – heavier than that of a private car – she knew it to be the ambulance.

Slipping into a dressing-gown she went to the window, wishing that she could get a cup of tea without going downstairs. She decided to do without it, and opened the door, intending to go along to the bathroom and have a cold shower.

Someone was coming up the stairs.

She could see the top of his head, before it disappeared at the bend in the stairs; the dark, wavy hair, and high forehead were unmistakable. There was a pleasant clinking sound, reminiscent of morning-tea.

'Are you awake, Mrs Fayne?' Frend called, tactfully pretending not to see her.

'Yes, of course,' answered Valerie, laughing.

Not until she had finished a second cup, and he had talked lightly about the events of the night, did Frend come to the real reason for his visit.

'Webb is going to ask you to see the body of the man they found outside, Mrs Fayne,' he said. 'No! please don't look like that!' She had paled, and her eyes had widened in alarm. 'It won't be very much of an ordeal. Webb has his job to do, and I understand that he arranged not to move the body till this morning, so that you could have some sleep before seeing it.'

It explained why Webb had stipulated eight o'clock for the ambulance; and she supposed that nothing could have saved her from going through with the unpleasant task. She pulled herself together; it would not be the first dead man she had seen, and there would be no personal grief to add poignancy to the incident.

'Of course. Is Webb in a hurry?'

'He would like you to come down as soon as possible.'

Every moment of delay made the prospect seem more

repugnant, and it was little more than five minutes afterwards that she went downstairs.

Frend was in the sitting-room and heard her coming. No one else was there. Smoking his large, charred pipe, he greeted her with his now familiar smile and led her along towards the kitchen and the little maid's room, where the body lay. Frend, nodding to the policeman standing by, tapped at the door.

Webb was alone in the room. The body, which was on the camp bed, had a sheet drawn over it. Valerie averted her eyes. Webb greeted her with a stiff 'Good-morning' and a formal apology for putting her through so unpleasant a task. Then, deliberately and slowly, so that she should not be taken unawares, he moved the sheet from the face, speaking as he did so:

'All I want to know, Mrs Fayne, is whether you know the man.'

The face, pale and small, with the eyes closed and the expression peaceful, lay revealed. It was the face of an old man – and it was not unfamiliar. She stared at it, open-mouthed and with her hands at her breast, momentarily oblivious of the gaze of the Inspector and the vicar.

Chapter 6

Identification

After a short pause, Webb looked away from her and drew the sheet back to its former position. Valerie felt the utter quietude of those who realise suddenly that they are in the mill of an inexorable fate, and there is nothing they can do about it.

It was Robin's Uncle Silas.

Had it not been for the portrait, she would have hesitated – seeing only a vague familiarity glimpsed by the photographs. But the portrait excluded all doubt.

Webb looked questioningly at her.

She nodded; her mouth was dry, and words were difficult to utter, but her voice was surprisingly steady.

'It is my husband's uncle, Silas Mottram. He owns the house. I don't think there can be any mistake. The – the portrait in the sitting-room.'

'I saw the likeness,' said Webb. 'Thank you very much. I won't need to trouble you any further now.' He nodded to Frend, and Valerie turned and went blindly out of the room. Battley was hovering near the kitchen door; neither he nor Valerie spoke as Frend led the way into the sitting-room.

The wind made the curtains billow into the room, but the cold breeze was only partly the cause of a shiver which ran through Valerie.

'What *can* it mean?' she asked, at last. 'Mr Frend, what is it all about?'

'We don't know yet,' said Frend quietly, 'and I don't think we're going to find out by making wild guesses!'

'Battley would know,' Valerie said.

'I expect Webb will realise that,' said Frend, 'Mrs Fayne, I don't think I need tell you that the identification alters the whole complexion of the affair.'

'I know it does,' said Valerie. 'Robin's uncle – murdered.' She looked up sharply. '*Is* it murder?'

Yes,' said Frend. 'But there are a variety of reasons for murder, and the theft of the portraits might have something to do with it. The police will find out whether they're valuable, and – '

'Please! exclaimed Valerie. 'I'm not fool enough to think that it could all be hushed up. He was a rich man, and – well, his heirs will benefit, won't they? Including Robin. And he was buried in the grounds here. That will make the police suspect the family and – Robin and I – ' she broke off. 'Am I being hysterical?'

Frend smiled.

'Certainly not! You're taking it very well.'

'Am I?' asked Valerie. 'I wonder?' She moved restlessly, unwilling to take even this crumb of comfort. 'I don't think I am,' she said. 'I suppose it's because I'm tired, and the damage in the orchard gave me such a shock.' She was speaking as much to herself as to Frend, 'I'm behaving like a frightened woman who can't face up to facts. Webb must think I'm half-way to being an idiot!' She drew a deep breath, and her smile grew more natural. 'Don't deny it! I have made a fool of myself, but I intend to stop forthwith. The first sensible thing to do is to telephone Robin. What time is it?'

'Half-past eight.'

After several irritating delays she managed to get connected to Robin's number – he was staying in a hotel at Oxford – but there was further delay after the hotel had answered. Then a distant voice told her that Mr Fayne had left ten minutes before.

Valerie replaced the receiver slowly.

'Well, that's that! – there's nothing to be done until tonight, when he'll be at Chester.'

'Have you no idea where he'll be during the day?' asked Frend.

'No, he wasn't sure.' She paused, and her eyes widened. 'I suppose the police will want to get in touch with him?'

'I shouldn't be surprised,' said Frend, gently, 'and with other relatives, too. Do you know them?'

'Not a single one,' said Valerie. 'Do you seriously think he'll – but of course he will!'

Her mind began to dwell on the relatives; Charles, Robin's brother, who was in the Navy; the cousins, William and Lynda. Robin had given her brief word-sketches of them all.

William, a barrister by profession, whom no-one would dream of calling 'Bill' because he was such a pontifical ass, but not, Robin had been careful to assure her, a fool; Lynda – a beauty, and already the heroine of a series of hectic love affairs.

All he had said of his brother was that Charles was 'all right'. He had talked very little about Charles, but Valerie believed that he was devoted to him, and concealed that devotion with a characteristic reserve. Of the three, only William was married, but he had no children. William was a Mottram, the last of the Mottrams in fact, so it was up to the Faynes to keep the family going. Robin had said that laughingly, but with an underlying note of seriousness.

All those thoughts and reflections had passed through Valerie's mind while Frend was standing and drawing at his empty pipe. With difficulty she forced her attention back to the present.

The immediate problem of keeping house was solved, for Battley had prepared breakfast for her; she had it in the morning-room, after Frend, firmly refusing to share it, had gone off.

The ambulance had also gone, with most of the police. There remained only Webb, Carrow, two other uniformed men and a plain clothes detective called Kennedy. Webb came in, and asked her how he could get in touch with Robin. She gave him the number of Robin's office, after telling him about the hotel; she would have preferred to break the news to Robin herself, but Webb made it clear that he preferred to do so, and she saw no way of forestalling him.

He seemed to be aiming at some point which he did not make clear, but before he went he dropped a hint that it was more than likely, indeed, desirable, that her husband's relations, when advised of the news, would come immediately to The Paddocks.

'My brother-in-law isn't likely to come,' Valerie told him. 'He's at sea, I think.'

'Actually, he is ashore,' said Webb.

After he had gone, the brief words 'actually, he is ashore' worried Valerie.

She tried to concentrate on the pending domestic problems, and discussed them all with Mrs North, who arrived punctually, agog at the happenings, some rumour of which had already reached the village.

The stout figure of Joe Parker appeared precariously astride her bicycle. Avidly fishing for news he said at last that he had heard of a 'gent's bike' which might be just what she wanted. He promised to let her have further particulars early in the afternoon.

Valerie had hardly got rid of him when a ring at the front door heralded the arrival of an elderly, untidy-looking man with a slight stammer, an apologetic manner, and the information that he represented the *Pelshire Gazette*.

No one had advised her what attitude to take with newspapermen, and this man's arrival made her realise that he was only the forerunner of others. She felt even more sure of that after the *Gazette* representative had made it clear that Uncle Silas had been a personality of some importance in London – a well-known clubman, a keen philatelist, and a dilettante who dabbled in the arts.

Not until the man had gone, did she appreciate that the murder of Silas Mottram was going to cause a sensation which would spread wider than Pelshire and the family. Unsure, uncertain what to do, she decided to telephone Webb.

Chief Inspector Webb – had Valerie looked at his card she would have seen that he was entitled to the 'Chief', although he had not used it when introducing himself – went from The Paddocks to his home on the outskirts of Listow. His wife, a long-suffering woman of great restraint, cooked his breakfast, laid out his shaving tackle, and waved him good-bye without once alluding to the obvious fact that he needed six hours uninterrupted sleep.

As he arrived at the headquarters of the Pelshire Constabulary and C.I.D. a sergeant on duty saluted. Webb nodded and hurried to his office. Here his own particular sergeant, Bennett, was looking through the Mottram files.

'Good-morning, sir! How are things going?' Bennett radiated that particular brand of optimism and good-will which, after a sleepless night, was more difficult to face than the deepest gloom.

'It's too early to say,' said Webb. 'Is the Colonel in yet?'

'He hasn't sent word, sir, and I've heard nothing.'

'Good! We should have half-an-hour to ourselves. Where are the files?'

There were three files finished, and a sheet of paper covered with Bennett's bold, legible hand-writing. He had been through all the details available on Silas Mottram and picked out the material points, numbering them.

By the time the Chief Inspector had finished with the files on Mottram, Robin Fayne, and Charles Fayne, Bennett had finished looking through those on William and Lynda Mottram. Webb glanced expectantly at the clock, for he was waiting for a summons from the Chief Constable – Colonel Malcolm Grey – at any moment. It was eleven o'clock, before the telephone rang. Webb picked it up:

'Webb speaking.'

'Come along now, will you?' It was Grey. 'Unless you're particularly busy, that is.'

'No, I'm quite ready, sir.' Webb collected the files and stood up, looking at Bennett. 'You're getting data about Mrs Fayne and the Derings, aren't you?'

'Yes, sir. There isn't much about Mrs Fayne I can get hold of, but London's promised to go into it and telephone through if there's anything of importance. She was a Miss Marshall, and worked in the same department as Mr Fayne, and they've only been married a week or two.'

'Yes I know,' said Webb. He looked thoughtful as he approached the door. 'Find out whether she is in any other way connected with the Mottram family. And – ' Webb narrowed his eyes – 'find out what she knows about painting. I want the information as quickly as possible. Keep worrying London for it.'

'Very good,' said Bennett, smiling.

His smile became a wide grin as the door closed. He rubbed his hands together. 'Cripes!' he exclaimed, 'he's got something! He's after Mrs Fayne!'

He reached out for the telephone.

Chapter 7

Webb Reports Fully

Colonel Grey was a man of medium height, with a deceptively mild air. His eyes were innocent of guile, and his voice quiet.

'Ah, Webb,' he said. 'Good-morning.'

'Good-morning, sir,' said Webb.

'Sit down.' Grey turned to his chair and lowered himself into it gently, as if he were afraid to make a sudden movement. 'You've been up all night, I suppose?' Webb nodded. 'How have you got on?'

'It's rather early to say yet, sir,' said Webb. 'We've found Mottram, of course – he was buried in the orchard at the house.'

'How was he found?'

'I heard that there had been some bother there – someone had cut the blossom off some of the trees – and I wondered if it was the senseless act it seemed. So I had the blossom cleared away, and we found that the turf had been dug up and carefully replaced. Mottram hadn't been there long. Dr Pemberton thinks he was murdered about midnight last night, and no one is likely to be more definite about the time.'

'How was Mottram killed?'

'He was stabbed in the back. The knife was still in the wound the hilt broken, or sawn off. There is a fraying on the back of the coat, suggesting that the handle was deliberately sawn off, after the crime.'

'Oh,' said Grey. 'Unusual?'

'Very, sir,' said Webb. 'Obviously it was an attempt to prevent us from identifying the knife. Equally, it's clear that whoever killed him wanted to prevent bleeding, in order to get him to the garden without leaving a trail.'

'From where?' asked Grey.

'I don't know yet,' said Webb. 'The most convenient place

would have been The Paddocks. There's a cottage about a hundred yards away from it, but no other house within a quarter of a mile.'

'So you think he was killed at The Paddocks?'

'I don't want to commit myself to an opinion yet, sir,' said Webb. 'There are a number of other things – '

He told Grey exactly what had happened, referring to pencilled notes from time to time. That part of his report was factual; he did not deal with any individuals, save to say what they had done. From it, however, there emerged the picture of a woman, young and attractive, who was hostile almost from the beginning, and had been antagonistic towards Carrow. That hostility grew more obvious as Webb's story developed. He expressed no opinion as to the cause of it.

Valerie's manner contrasted with that of Frend, who was anxious to be helpful, and with that of Battley, who was non-committal as far as Webb was concerned, although he bore no love for Carrow because of the old-standing feud between them.

When the narration was finished, Grey began to toy with a pencil.

'Very comprehensive, Webb! The theft of the pictures is curious, to say the least. Rather peculiar, don't you think, that Mrs Fayne suspected there was somebody in the house, but did not mention the fact?'

'I do think it's peculiar,' admitted Webb. 'On the other hand, she took a dislike to me.' His expression did not alter. 'It may have been just that.'

'It may also have been that she had some reason to be afraid of you,' said Grey. 'H'm, yes. If she knew that the body was there, she would be frightened. If she were frightened, then she would have a good reason for being hostile.' Grey smiled, unexpectedly. 'But I won't ask you for an opinion, yet! You know, don't you, that this case will cause quite a stir? Silas Mottram was a character, and not unknown in government circles.' Grey's manner of speaking implied an understatement. 'He was a wealthy man with a mean streak, and he had several relatives who, if not exactly poor, could do with more money. You're getting in touch with each one, of course.'

'I'm trying to get them all here,' said Webb. 'I think we shall manage it. It's lucky that Charles Fayne is ashore. Still, if he'd been at sea, he would have been out of the running. Incidentally, I have already discovered that he's in the hands of money-lenders. Not for a large amount – about three hundred pounds – but it shows the way the wind blows.'

'He would find his share of Mottram's fortune very useful,' mused Grey. 'I daresay the others would do too. You know, Webb, it's a peculiar affair in many ways.'

Webb waited, tactfully.

'*Most* peculiar,' continued Grey. 'You remember that the first we heard of it was when Mottram applied to Scotland Yard for protection. Fortunately the Yard sent us a note of it, since Mottram was a land-owner down here. Then he had a most important appointment – let me see, when was it?'

'Two days ago,' said Webb, 'for Sunday evening.'

'Why any man has to choose a Sunday evening for an appointment with his solicitor, it's hard to say,' said Grey, 'except that it makes it fairly certain that the matter was urgent. According to the report we had, the Yard was informed when Mottram failed to turn up. The Yard knew within two hours, and we knew first thing on Monday morning. H'm, yes. Mottram's appeal for protection and the fact that he thought he might be attacked made us – and the Yard – think he might have been killed. And it was so! On the whole, Webb, I think the Yard will compliment you on the speed with which you worked. And they should!'

'Thank-you, sir. But the idiot who cut the blossom off the trees really put the whole thing in my hands,' Webb said. 'It was obviously an attempt to hide the fact that the turf had been disturbed, and it might have succeeded had the blossom been left there – it would have given the murderer time to formulate his plans, at all events.'

'You've no idea at all who cut the blossom?'

'Not yet,' said Webb. 'Anyone in Pelham had the opportunity, and the night was perfect for it. The Faynes' could have done it themselves, but if they had, would Mrs Fayne have reported to the police so promptly?'

'The fact that the blossom had been cut off would have gone round the village like wildfire,' said Grey knowledgeably, 'and in my opinion she would have roused more suspicion by failing to report it than by getting into touch with our man at Pelham. No real indication either way there, I think. Well, now, what about the others?'

'We've discussed Charles Fayne,' said Webb. 'As for William Mottram, it's hardly conceivable. He's well-known, and he's the only one of the family wealthy enough to be fairly indifferent to his uncle's money. On the other hand, he and his uncle were on bad terms. We don't yet know why, but probably it was a family feud of some kind. His sister, Lynda, has a reputation of being fast – and she's something of a beauty. She has been concerned in one or two scandals, including a breach of promise.'

Grey raised one eyebrow.

'Did she win?'

'Yes.' Webb was brusque. 'She was awarded a thousand pounds and costs, but that was four years ago. She runs an expensive flat in London, and by all accounts she doesn't practise economy.'

'How old is she?'

'Twenty-five.'

'H'm. She's obviously managed to move about a bit in her quarter of a century! Well, Webb, where else are you looking?'

'I've asked Scotland Yard for a copy of their file on Mottram,' said Webb, 'and they've promised to send it down. They've kept pretty close at the Yard, so far.' He smiled, wryly. 'I expect they're waiting for us to call them in.'

Grey eyed him steadily, and asked:

'Are we going to?'

'That's up to you, sir.'

'Is it?' asked Grey. 'I wonder! If you think you've a fair chance of getting results yourself in a few days – well, I'd like to feel that we handled it without any assistance. On the other hand, if we have to call them in later, they'll complain that we've let the trail go cold. Ought we to take the risk?'

'I don't think I'd let myself be swayed by that consideration, sir, but – it is a fact that the Yard has already been working on Mottram. They might insist on calling it their case. Even if not, they may have something which they'll share with us if we ask them for help, but will keep back unless – or until – we do.'

'In other words, you think we ought to ask them right away, but you don't want to ask them at all! That about sums it up, doesn't it? And mine is the casting vote.' Grey shrugged. 'We'd better have them, Webb. I'm sorry, but – '

'On the whole, I think its best, sir,' said Webb.

'Good!' Grey was brisk. 'I'll get in touch with them at once. There's nothing else you want at the moment, is there? Then go home and get some sleep!'

Leaving the Chief Constable's office with an unreasonable sense of depression – for it was, after all, largely at his own wish that Scotland Yard was being called in – Webb caught up with Dr Pemberton. He had lost no time in doing the post-mortem, but there was nothing fresh to report.

'The clothes I've left to you,' Pemberton said, 'not that you'll get much from them, after his spell under the apple-tree. Bizarre kind of imagination, whoever did that!'

'I suppose so,' admitted Webb, absently. 'I say, Pemberton – you knew Dering pretty well, didn't you?'

'I did, yes. Why?'

'I didn't know him at all,' said Webb. 'But I heard some gossip a week or two ago. Apparently he decided to get out of The Paddocks at pretty short notice.'

'He did,' said Pemberton. 'In fact, he had promised to give a talk to the Horticultural Society. He didn't have the courtesy to cancel it.'

'Oh.' Webb surveyed the rugged face in front of him. 'Curious,' he said. 'Do you know anything about the despoiling of his orchids? There were one or two other incidents in the garden while he was there, weren't there?'

'There was an outbreak of vandalism in and around Pelham,' said Pemberton. 'You know that as well as I do – what are you getting at? I don't think the trouble Dering had was any different from that at the Vicarage and the other large houses. A senseless business! If I were you, I'd watch old Battley. He hated the sight of Dering, and – '

Pemberton stopped abruptly, as if he wished he had not gone so far, but was now unable to retract.

'Oh, well, I suppose I'd better pass on the local gossip. It was said that Battley and Dering's gardener were at daggers drawn, and that Battley interfered with the brakes of the gardener's bike one day, when he knew he was going down Fork Hill. Only rumour, mind – well I'll be getting along.'

Webb delayed going home for five minutes, while he instructed Bennett to find out where the previous tenant had gone after leaving The Paddocks, and to get what information he could about him.

He was troubled by Dering's sudden departure from The Paddocks, and the possibility that someone besides Mottram's relatives might be concerned.

Home at last, he left instructions that he was not to be called until five o'clock except for developments of outstanding urgency.

Webb went to sleep.

He was awakened just after half-past four, having slept for a little less than three hours, by hearing his wife talking to Bennett in the passage. He struggled up to a sitting position as the door opened. Bennett was beaming happily, quite oblivious of his superior's displeasure.

'Well, what is it?' growled Webb.

'I thought you ought to know, sir,' said Bennett, with deep satisfaction, 'that Kennedy has just rung up from The Paddocks. He's found out where the old boy was killed.'

Det. Sergeant Kennedy was a bumptious and self-advertising individual whom Webb and most of the men at the station heartily disliked.

To do Webb justice, he was not prejudiced by Kennedy's braggadocio; his chief complaint was that Kennedy did the obvious things well enough, but was incapable of constructive thinking, while there were times when the sergeant took a matter into his own hands and made a howling mess of it. To all Webb's reprimands, Kennedy presented an aggrieved face, afterwards complaining bitterly of the Chief Inspector's jealousy.

It was Kennedy's strong belief that one day he would make a discovery of such importance that promotion could no longer be denied him. In the case of Silas Mottram this expectation ran high.

He prided himself on his discretion, and it was true that Valerie did not find him too much in the way, and was not, in fact, even aware that he was in the attic.

'In my opinion,' declared Kennedy, surveying the attic in the manner of an admiral reviewing a not too well disciplined fleet, 'this is the most likely place for the murder to have been committed. What's that on the floor?'

The plain clothes man looked at a thin layer of sawdust on the floor, and said:

'Mouse-droppings, probably.'

'I disagree!' said Kennedy sharply. He pulled up the legs

of his well-creased trousers, and bent down, stirring the stuff with his finger. It was just beneath the skylight. 'This is sawdust, Green!'

Green said nothing.

'If I remember rightly,' went on Kennedy, 'the handle of the knife which was used to kill Silas Mottram was sawn off. This is most important.' He took an envelope from his pocket and put a few grains of the sawdust in it, then straightened up and looked about him again, with narrowed eyes. Suddenly, he pounced on something else on the floor, and ten minutes later he moved an old picture frame and came upon an object which raised his expectation to the supreme pitch.

Soon he was downstairs at the telephone, barely able to restrain his annoyance because – as *usual*, he later told Green – Webb was not at the office, and he was forced to pass on his splendid news to that grinning ass Bennett.

Chapter 8

Robin hears the News

Drowsiness and annoyance vanishing simultaneously, as Webb said sharply to Bennett:

'Was he killed at the house?'

'Right, first go!' said Bennett, disappointed yet admiring. 'In the attic. Kennedy found two or three spots of blood – microscopic, he said they were – *and* the handle of the knife!'

'What?' exclaimed Webb, getting out of bed.

'No doubt at all about it, sir,' said Bennett. 'The murderer had some nerve. Kennedy says he's found the saw that did it in the kitchen at The Paddocks. Kennedy's pretty good, isn't he?' Bennett added with sly innocence.

'He's a paragon,' grunted Webb.

Bennett hid a smile. 'It looks as if we might be able to have it all settled by the time the men come from the Yard.' Bennett sniffed. 'That would give them something to think about!'

Webb ignored that pious hope, and said:

'I'll go out and have a look at The Paddocks myself.'

He was dressed by the time his wife had made some tea, and, half-an-hour after Bennett's visit, was on his way to The Paddocks. As he neared Pelham, he saw Frend and Mrs Fayne talking outside the vicarage gate. Mrs Fayne looked up as he drew nearer, and he wondered if it was fear that he read in her expression.

Robin Fayne's position in the Air Ministry was one of considerable – if dubious – opportunity. He was a liaison officer working between the Ministry and the privately-owned factories. In the course of the past two years, he might, had he so chosen, have greatly profited, for profits ran high and the goodwill of influential officers was valuable. To all offers, however, he turned a deaf ear. He watched production carefully, with intelligence and integrity, and was popular both at the Ministry and with his commercial acquaintances.

As a bachelor, he had lived within his income, but his job and his habit of paying legitimate working expenses out of his own pocket – a *laissez-faire* attitude which would have to stop now that he was married – had not allowed him a great margin. His bank balance stood at a little under five hundred pounds and his income, if wisely used, would meet his domestic expenses.

When he heard that The Paddocks was available, he had not been able to resist it, although – meeting his cousin Lynda purely by chance – he had expressed himself strongly over the exorbitance of the rent.

His brother, Charles, was in a different category.

Charles had brought his submarine safely to a Scottish port, where it was undergoing repairs. He had wired to Robin, suggesting a meeting somewhere in the North – or so Robin had told Graham Wells, a colleague at the Ministry – and they had arranged to meet at the hotel in Chester.

When Wells received the message from the Pelshire police, he immediately telephoned the firm where Robin was due to make his last call. But Robin had left, shortly before, expressing the intention of going to the Chester hotel.

Robin was alone in the hotel lounge, when he was summoned to the telephone.

He had received a message from Charles, who was due there at six o'clock, and it was then a little after four.

'Hallo,' he said, into the telephone. 'Hallo – who? . . . Oh, Wells! Now what?'

'Robin, I've a message for you which will probably be a bit of a shock.'

'Why, what's wrong? Not the Ajax business? I thought that had worked itself out.'

'It's a private matter,' said Wells. He sounded diffident. 'I had a message from the Pelshire Police.' Once started, he continued quickly. 'An uncle of yours – Silas Mottram – do you know him?'

'Don't be an ass!' said Robin, 'of course I do.'

'Well, he's been murdered.'

'*What's* that?'

'Confound you, listen to what I'm saying!' said Wells, fretfully. 'Your Uncle Silas has been – well, he's dead! I gathered that the police suspect foul play. Beastly message to have to pass on, old man, but – well, there you are!'

'But I tell you I saw Uncle Silas only a fortnight ago,' boomed Robin. 'He was full of beans with every prospect of living to be an octogenarian!'

'This isn't a joke,' protested Wells. 'You're wanted back at Pelham as quickly as you can get there. I promised that you should have the message tonight. Robin, it's a fact!'

After a pause, Robin said:

'So I'm just beginning to believe.'

'Can I do anything? Send messages, or anything like that?'

'I don't think so,' said Robin slowly. 'Oh yes! Yes, get someone else to do my calls for me tomorrow, will you? Or else cancel my engagements. And tell the old man what's happened. I'll get in touch with him as soon as I can. Good-bye, old chap. Many thanks.'

Robin replaced the receiver, and stood jingling some coins in his pocket. He was frowning, and a lock of upstanding hair, casually out of place, gave him a youthful appearance, belied by his expression.

He booked a call to The Paddocks and strolled moodily into the lounge, wishing that the bar was open. He had ordered tea, when the telephone rang.

'Your call to Pelham 16, sir. Hold on, please.'

Robin's heart was beginning to beat faster; it always did when he was telephoning Valerie. He felt guilty because, after two attempts, he had given up trying to ring her the previous evening.

Then a man spoke:

'This is Pelham 16.'

'Who is that?' asked Robin, sharply. 'Is Mrs Fayne there?'

'No, sir,' said the man. 'She is out at the moment.'

'Then who are you?' demanded Robin.

'I am a police officer, sir. Can I give Mrs Fayne a message?' The man sounded disinterested.

Robin drew a hand across his forehead, trying to compose himself. The last shred of doubt had gone; Wells had been right, and foul play was obviously suspected.

'Ye-es,' he said slowly. 'Tell her that I called – I'm Mr Fayne – and that I will ring through again if possible, otherwise I shall probably be on the way home.'

'Very good, sir.'

'Tell her that I doubt whether I can get home tonight,' went on Robin, 'but I shall certainly arrive early tomorrow morning. Have you got that?'

'Yes, sir. I will tell her as soon as she comes in.'

He rang off, lit a cigarette, and finished a cup of tea that had gone cold.

He realised, with a shock, that he was not distressed at the news of his uncle's death.

He ruminated on that for some time, then calculated the chances of getting to Pelham that night. He could not leave before Charles arrived – Charles would come with him, he felt sure – which meant that it would be impossible to reach Pelham before two o'clock; if Charles wanted a meal, it would be nearer three.

Looking out of the window, he saw a taxi draw up, and the emerging figure of his brother.

Dashing out of the room, he reached the pavement as Charles, in the naval uniform of a Lieutenant-Commander, turned to greet him.

'Hallo, old boy!' Charles crushed Robin's fingers. 'Hallo, then! I call this a true brotherly greeting!'

'Damn your eyes!' said Robin, half-laughing, 'it's always good to see you. How are you?'

'*I'm* all right,' said Charles. 'You're the ailing one – where's your schoolboy complexion? Doesn't marriage agree with you? You told me that –'

'Hush!' exclaimed Robin.

By then, carrying a valise apiece, they were in the foyer of the hotel, and the old porter was approaching.

'Are you particularly hungry?' asked Robin.

'No, I had a late lunch and an early tea, and caught a faster train than I expected.'

'Shall I take your cases up, sir?' asked the porter.

Robin answered for his brother.

'No, we'll keep them down here.' He waited until the old man was out of earshot, and then grinned at Charles. 'You nearly lost a point, old man – no confidences within anyone's hearing!'

'You can carry a joke too far,' said Charles, lightly. He looked into Robin's eyes. 'What's on your mind, Robin? You don't look yourself.'

Robin said slowly:

'I don't feel it. Charles, we might be in a spot. It's just as well that nobody knows that it's only a day or so since I saw you.'

'Out with it!' exhorted Charles.

Robin plunged into the story. As soon as murder was mentioned, Charles stopped smiling, and he listened without interrupting, his face unusually grave.

Robin took out his cigarette case as he finished.

'And that's all I know. I couldn't get anything out of the policeman who was on the phone – it rather bowled me over, anyhow.'

'It is a bit staggering,' said Charles, his voice remarkably mild. 'And damned awkward too, old chap.'

'Awkward's the word,' admitted Robin.

'It happened on Monday night?'

'It must have done,' Robin said. 'Thereabouts, anyhow – we've got some thinking to do, and we'd better make it good!'

'You're the brain-merchant,' Charles said, offhandedly.

'You'll come down with me, won't you?' asked Robin. 'I think we'd better stop *en route*. Let's see – ' He glanced at his watch. 'It's getting on for five. We should get pretty well as far as Bath by ten o'clock, and we can leave about five in the morning and get home before ten. Is that all right with you?'

'Anything you say,' said Charles, helpfully.

Robin became aware of a peculiar fact; Charles had not made any comment on the fact that Uncle Silas had been murdered.

A little after five they started out, Robin at the wheel, and Charles sitting next to him and whistling softly under his breath. The shock had passed, but still he did not mention Uncle Silas, talking only of their own situation.

The fact began to prey on Robin's mind.

Chapter 9

Lynda

A shaft of sunlight, shining through the branches of the beech trees on the drive, caught the face of the woman who was walking towards The Paddocks. Her hair, very fair and beautifully coiffured, gleamed in the sun. She walked with a steady, easy stride, carrying a small travelling case. Valerie, watching from the porch, saw that she was not only well turned-out, she was beautiful. As Valerie hurried forward, she put the case down by her side and drew a deep breath.

'Thank goodness I'm here! You're Valerie, of course?'

'Yes. You're Lynda?'

'Yes. I *knew* Robin would know what he was about!'

The smiling, charming compliment brought a flush of pleasure to Valerie's cheeks. I'm going to like her, she thought.

'Couldn't you get a taxi?' she asked. 'If I'd known, I would have arranged for one to meet the train.'

'If Robin's had time to mention me yet,' said Lynda, laughingly, 'you'll know that I never tell anyone in advance when I'm likely to arrive – I never know myself!'

Battley appeared, with his usual soundlessness, and relieved Valerie of the case.

'A retainer already?' said Lynda. 'Haven't I seen him before? He seems familiar. Val, what a divine place this is!' She stood looking at the front of the house, her appreciation obviously sincere. 'I've not been here much – my father was never very family conscious – but it always has a soothing effect on me. But of course, it's new to you. Where's Robin?'

'Away,' said Valerie awkwardly.

Lynda threw her glance heavenward. 'This upheaval! and Robin chasing about the country! One thing's certain; he'll be back as soon as he hears what's happened.' That was her first oblique reference to Uncle Silas, and she added with a gleam in her eyes: 'You'll soon get tired of talking about the unpleasant details. Has it been too bad?'

'We-ell, it was a shock. The – ' Valerie hesitated, wondering how Lynda would react to the mention of Frend – 'the local vicar has been a tower of strength.'

'Some are, aren't they?' said Lynda, as they went up the stairs. 'Though I always find towers rather depressing. Nothing's changed, I see. I'm glad the old place is back in the family, it seemed wrong to have strangers living here.'

Her case was already in one of the spare rooms, opposite the bathroom. Valerie left her to make sure that everything was ready. Mrs North had stayed until late afternoon, and Battley had ordained to remain at the house until Robin returned. His presence was welcome, although three policement were still on the premises.

Valerie had no idea of the discovery in the attic, or that the house had been thoroughly searched in her absence. She had received the message from Robin, and had been keenly disappointed at being out when he had phoned. There had been a telegram from William Mottram, to say he would be arriving some time that day. So far, she had had no word from Charles.

There had been plenty to keep her occupied, and she found it easy not to think too much about the murder. Frend and his sister had not talked about it during her second visit to the Vicarage, but Lynda, with her frank directness of approach, was another matter.

Over supper Valerie found herself relating exactly what had happened, and when she had finished, Lynda said, thoughtfully:

'It's the very devil, isn't it? Hadn't you any idea that Silas was in the neighbourhood?'

'Not the faintest,' Valerie assured her.

'He always was a secretive old curmudgeon. Imagine anyone to whom "curmudgeon" applies, double it, and you've got him!'

'So you didn't like him?' said Valerie.

'No one *liked* Silas,' said Lynda, reflectively, 'he was too full of moral righteousness. Do I shock you, talking about him like this?' Valerie shook her head.

'People don't change because they are dead.'

'No, but it is a convention to pretend they do, and I've never been very good at conforming to conventions. I'm so glad you approve, you know I had a dreadful fear, when I heard that Robin was married, that the lure might have been his imaginary fortune!' She looked up, startled. 'You *know* he's not exactly a Croesus, don't you?'

'I know all the risks,' said Valerie lightly.

'That's a relief! No one taught me tact. Robin has it all, I think – William puts his foot in it every time he has a chance.'

'What about Charles?' asked Valerie.

'Ah, Charles! You don't know him, either?' Although she smiled, there was a change in Lynda's expression. 'Oh, Charles is all right, only one never sees him. You'll like Charles. Do you know why the police wanted us to come down here?'

Without waiting for an answer she changed the subject quickly, chatting easily until dusk fell and they went round the house drawing the curtains. Valerie suggested a walk in the grounds, and whistling Jinx to follow them, they strolled through the orchard until it was too dark to see their way.

Returning, it was Lynda who caught sight of something white on the hall mat. As Valerie closed the door, Lynda picked up a sealed envelope. It was quite plain, frowning, she handed it to Valerie. There was a single sheet of folded paper inside – of thick, fairly good quality.

There was no address and no signature, and it ran:

'Don't think you can get away with it, Mrs Fayne. So you're a stranger here, are you? I don't think!'

That was all.

Valerie read it again, her lips tightening. Lynda who had moved to the piano, glanced over her shoulder saying:

'What is it?'

'It's absurd!' said Valerie, the colour gone from her cheeks. 'I – look, read it!'

Lynda took the letter:

'Someone's suffering from delusions!' Her eyes ran quickly over Valerie. 'What black past are you hiding Mrs Fayne?' She re-folded the paper. 'Anonymous letters are about the beastliest kind of approach I know – I had a spate of them once. Someone thought I was trying to break up a happy home! Don't look so bewildered, Val!'

'But I *am* bewildered,' said Valerie. 'Of course I'm a stranger here – '

'Of course,' echoed Lynda. 'What are you going to do? Burn it? Or keep it for Robin? *He'll* make things hum when he gets here. Is there any chance of his arriving tonight, do you know?'

'It isn't likely,' said Valerie. 'I don't quite know what to do. I – oh!'

The front door bell pealed suddenly, shrilly.

Going into the hall she wondered whether the caller could be another newspaperman.

She opened the door, faced by utter darkness, although a faint light shone from the lounge, she felt her pulse quickening, for whoever was there did not speak.

'Who is it?' she asked.

There was no answer.

'Who is it?' Her voice rose a shade, and she was glad to hear Lynda's steps approaching.

No response came to her second question, and Lynda fumbled for the switch and pressed it down. Light flooded the hall and the porch, as well as the carriage way – but no one was there.

'It *was* the front door bell!' said Valerie. She advanced a step, and kicked against something which was lying on the ground.

'Steady!' warned Lynda.

Valerie looked down, and saw a small square parcel near the wall. It was neatly wrapped and sealed. She picked it up, stared along the silent drive.

Lynda drew her back and closed the door. Returning to the sitting-room she eyed the parcel curiously. It was about the size of a box containing a hundred cigarettes. Red sealing wax had been liberally applied, but, like the letter, the parcel bore no address.

'More anonymity,' said Lynda; her lightness seemed forced and a little overdone. 'Darling, do you think it could possibly be an *infernal machine?*'

Valerie made no answer to that flight of fancy, but broke the seals. There were two wrappings of brown paper, and then a tin box. Stuck to the lid of the tin, was a plain card with some lettering on it. It read:

'This will interest you *Mrs Fayne.*'

Valerie began to detach the adhesive tape with unsteady hands. Lynda watched her closely.

The tape did not come away easily; Valerie had only just prised up enough to get a firm grip, when the front door bell rang again.

Chapter 10

Webb is Aggressive

This time they went out together, leaving the light on when they opened the door. Chief Inspector Webb, stood there, blinking in the sudden glare.

In spite of the scare of the second ring, Valerie was relieved to see him. She introduced Lynda, who eyed the policeman curiously. Webb's shrewd gaze appraised her, as he bowed a formal acknowledgement. Then he spoke briskly.

'I would like a few words with you, Mrs Fayne.'

If he noticed the letter and the package, he made no comment.

'I'm sure Miss Mottram will excuse me if I say that I want to speak to you alone,' he said.

Lynda said dryly:

'There's something we want to talk about first. Valerie was just going to telephone you.'

'Indeed?' Webb sounded sceptical. 'What about, Mrs Fayne?'

'This,' said Valerie, picking up the letter, 'and this.' She indicated the unopened tin. 'The first was put in the letter box, the second was left on the doorstep, and whoever left it there rang the bell and ran away.'

Webb read the notes impassively, made no comment, and then pulled at the adhesive tape, but the lid did not come up easily. He gave all his attention to the task, and the two women watched him closely. Valerie was the first to see the contents of the box.

It was a black Moroccan leather case.

'Curiouser and curiouser,' said Lynda, irrepressibly.

They could see that it was a jewel case and Valerie wondered if she looked as surprised as she felt, as Webb opened it. Again she was the first to see the contents.

'Well, well!' said Lynda, her voice unnaturally controlled. 'A belated wedding-present, Val?'

Impassively, Webb took a diamond necklace from the velvet bed, and held it up to the light, scintillations gleamed from the facets, reducing the rest of the room to shadow. None of them spoke for an appreciable time – in fact, not until Webb replaced the necklace, leaving the case open on the table.

'A somewhat unusual gift,' he commented, dryly. 'Have you seen it before?'

'No,' said Valeria; the word stuck in her throat.

'Yes,' said Lynda.

She picked the necklace up, looking at it more closely. 'At least, I think I have,' she amended. She began to count the stones. 'Six – seven – eight,' counted Lynda. 'One in the middle, nine – ' she went on counting up to seventeen, and then said quietly: 'Yes, I have – if it's real. Would you be able to tell, Inspector?'

'I think it's real,' said Webb. 'Why do you think it might be paste?'

'If I had a necklace worth ten thousand pounds, I wouldn't leave it on the doorstep,' Lynda said, 'but you never can tell with people, can you?'

'Where have you seen it before?' asked Webb, stolidly.

'On my grandmother's bosom,' said Lynda.

Valerie exclaimed: 'You mean it's – '

'A family heirloom,' Lynda completed for her. 'Yes, there isn't any doubt about that. It belonged to Uncle Silas. I suppose it's a moot point who owns it now!'

Webb looked disapproving, but all he said was:

'We shall know in good time who it belongs to, Miss Mottram. Was there anything written on the package, Mrs Fayne?'

Valerie picked up the note which had been stuck to the lid of the tin, and turned it over. There were two lines, in block lettering. She read them quickly, her colour heightening as she did so. Webb's gaze had never seemed so intent nor so suspicious.

'May I?' He stretched out a hand, and Valerie let him take the slip. She watched him, as he read aloud in a monotonous and stilted voice: *'If you keep silent, so shall I. Such necklaces don't grow on trees.'*

Webb's gaze changed, becoming very cold:

'I think that it is time we had that talk, Mrs Fayne. Do you mind leaving us, Miss Mottram?'

Bewildered at every turn, Valerie steeled herself for the coming interview. She told herself that she must not panic, but she got very near to it. Everything that had happened enmeshed her yet further. She could see a dozen indications that she was implicated in Uncle Silas's murder. Flat denials – all she could give – would make little impression on Webb.

Lynda broke a short silence. 'I am not unfamiliar with police procedure, Inspector, and I think I will stay.' Her eyes were mocking. 'I was once engaged to the son of Sir Roger Wilding, who, in case you are unaware of it, was the Chief Commissioner at Scotland Yard. It was a long time ago, but I feel sure that it isn't legal for you to *insist* on interviewing a witness without a third party present.'

Webb looked slightly uncomfortable.

'It may not be strictly legal to enforce it, Miss Mottram, but it might be wise for Mrs Fayne to make the concession.'

'I was never renowned for my wisdom,' said Lynda, lightly. 'What do you say, Val? If you'd rather I stay, stay I shall.'

'Stay, please,' said Valerie.

Webb shrugged his shoulders in acceptance. He had realised at once that it was going to be more difficult to deal with Lynda Mottram than with Mrs Fayne, and he wished the girl had not arrived. On the other hand, she was quite right. If he tried to exert pressure, he would lay himself open to reprimand, and, if Mrs Fayne should be held for trial, it would put a powerful weapon into the hands of the defence.

Valerie felt a surge of relief. She was full of admiration for Lynda's easy manner and the way she took control of the situation.

'There are one or two questions,' Webb began stiffly, 'that I would like to ask –'

'Will you smoke?' asked Lynda, holding out a cigarette case.

Webb's expression hardened; then he smiled, his tactics suddenly, suavely, altered. 'Thank you.' He lit her cigarette as well as his own. 'You don't mind if I continue now?'

'Please do,' said Lynda, faintly.

'Now, Mrs Fayne. You understand that an inquiry has to be held into the death of Mr Mottram. You know, of course, that he was murdered?'

'I'd guessed,' said Valerie, her face as wiped of expression as she could make it.

'He was murdered,' Webb said, flatly, 'in this house.'

Valerie started and Lynda dropped her cigarette.

'*Here*!' exclaimed Valerie. 'But it's impossible!'

'It happened,' said Webb, 'and it happened about midnight the night before last. You were here, I understand?'

'Yes, but – '

'Who was with you?'

'My husband. But – '

'Kindly restrict yourself to answering my questions,' said Webb, his voice uncompromisingly official. 'You and your husband were in the house at the time of the murder. Who else was here?'

'As far as I know, no one,' said Valerie.

'Can't you be sure?' Webb paused. 'It is usual for a hostess to know whether or not she has guests, Mrs Fayne. Who else was here?'

'If there were any others, I knew nothing of it – nor did my husband.'

'I'll be glad if you confine yourself to answering for *yourself*,' said Webb, sharply. 'I hope you are telling the truth, Mrs Fayne.'

'I am telling you the truth,' Valerie said, stiffly. She was pale, though not with anger. She recognised the danger, which was closing about her from all sides. Every moment seemed to make it more imminent. 'If anyone else were here on Monday night, it was without my knowledge.'

Webb snapped:

'You must have known that Silas Mottram was here!'

'I did not.'

'Mrs Fayne – ' Webb paused dramatically, drawling his words, 'are you seriously trying to tell me that a man who was afterwards murdered in one of the rooms of your house entered without your knowledge? He stayed here – ate here – talked here – all without your knowing?'

'I don't believe he did,' said Valerie, flatly.

'I must remind you that these facts are firmly established. But if it is true that you did not know he was here – you must have been very obtuse. Or did you turn a blind eye to – '

Valerie said:

'Inspector Webb, if you persist in such innuendo, I shall ask you to leave my house.'

Her words, grave and clear, took Webb completely by surprise.

He said, a little awkwardly,

'If I am mistaken, Mrs Fayne, I will certainly apologise. But I have reason to believe that Mr Silas Mottram was here on Monday evening. He was seen in the village. He was seen to enter the grounds of this house. He was killed here, and he was buried here. It is reasonable to assume that you and your husband know something about his visit. I am making no accusation, but I must ask for a full explanation of the facts. The absence of such an explanation will obviously give cause for suspicion.'

'I knew nothing about it,' said Valerie. 'Even now, I can't believe it to be true.'

But something had happened to her.

She spoke in a quieter voice and with nothing like the confidence with which she had faced Webb a few seconds before. She continued to look at him with clear, unwavering eyes, but some light had gone from them. She knew that Webb would notice the change, but she could do nothing to hide it, for she had remembered, with a vividness which shocked and frightened her, that Robin had stayed up until after midnight on the Monday evening.

During the day, she had spent too much time in the sun, and had developed a headache. Robin had letters to write. So she had gone upstairs soon after the nine o'clock news. She had gone to sleep, too, and when he had come to bed, she had been disturbed only enough to ask him the time. She could hear his voice ringing in her ears now:

'A little past twelve, darling. How's the head?'

'*A little past twelve*'; and he had been downstairs alone – or so she had thought – from about nine-fifteen.

Webb said:

'You appear to have recollected something, Mrs Fayne? Can you have remembered seeing Mr Mottram?'

'I didn't see him!' flared Valerie. 'He wasn't here – he couldn't have been!'

But she had reached breaking point, and Webb, sensing it, began to ply her with question after question, urging her, harassing her.

Lynda, sensing that Valerie must fight this out unaided, remained by her side, silent and motionless.

Chapter 11

Tense Struggle

Valerie thought:

'I mustn't let him know that Robin was downstairs without me.'

That thought guided her answers and explained the tenacity of her resistance. Had there been any admission to make, no matter how incriminating, she would probably have made it. As it was, although Webb fired the questions at her without remission, he could not guess what was really on her mind.

He maintained the pressure for a quarter-of-an-hour; then it was Lynda, not Valerie who could stand it no longer.

She sprang to her feet.

'Have you the right to badger her like this?' she demanded, angrily.

'I have every right to ask questions,' said Webb, coldly.

'I'll find out,' said Lynda. 'I don't think you have.'

Webb knew there was nothing she could do, and that he had kept strictly within his right; but she had broken the spell and given her companion breathing space.

'Have you anything to drink, Val?'

'There's whisky, and – '

'It doesn't matter,' said Lynda, restlessly. 'I really mean tea or coffee, but I won't leave Webb in here with you alone. How much longer are you staying, Inspector?'

'I haven't finished yet,' said Webb, grimly.

'Battley will probably be in the kitchen,' said Valerie. 'Ring and see.'

Not until Battley had answered the bell and gone off to make some tea, did Webb return to the attack. Having lost the advantage, he made no effort to regain it on the lines on which he had succeeded before. He switched to a fresh angle, quietly but intently.

'There is another matter, Mrs Fayne. When did you first come to Pelham?'

'I first came here about three weeks ago, and spent one night at The Angel,' said Valerie, steadily. 'A little more than a week later, I came here to live.'

'I see. You had never been here before?'

'I had not.'

'You are quite sure?'

'Of course I'm sure.'

Webb ignored her exasperation, and continued smoothly:

'How many people who live in Pelham did you know before you visited the village?'

'None.'

'Now, come!' remonstrated Webb. 'You can't expect me to believe that!'

Valerie eyed him stonily,

'I've given up expecting you to believe the truth, Inspector, you appear to live in a dream-world of your own.'

Webb looked so taken aback that Lynda laughed; and then, with another of those remarkable changes, without any indication that it was about to come, Webb joined in the laugh against himself.

'I mustn't build up that kind of reputation,' he said, almost gaily. 'Are you quite sure everyone in Pelham is a stranger to you?'

'Yes, everyone.'

'Even Battley?'

'Good heavens, yes!'

'Either you are completely hoodwinking me,' said Webb, in his more friendly voice, 'or else someone else is doing so, Mrs Fayne. The note you received this evening – how do you explain that?'

'I can't explain it. I'm not even going to try.'

'And the diamonds?'

'The same applies. Of course,' said Valerie, thawing a little, 'the diamonds are quite fantastic.' Her eyes strayed towards them. 'I wonder – ' she paused, then went on in a low-pitched voice: 'I wonder if anyone *thinks* that I have been here? That might explain it, mightn't it?'

Webb regarded her with narrowed eyes. Before he spoke, however, Battley came in with the tea.

'Thank you, Battley,' said Valerie, who could not quite believe in the old man, or in his position, which seemed to have become in a matter of hours that of an old and trusted servitor.

Valerie stepped past Webb towards the table and pushed the necklace aside to make room for the tray.

Battley stopped dead. His eyes widened, and Webb went forward swiftly, shooting out both hands to stop the tray from falling. But for his timely action it must have gone, for Battley's hands dropped to his sides, and he stared at the diamonds, an expression in his eyes closely akin to horror.

No one spoke; Webb stood with the tray in his hands, regarding the old man expressionlessly.

Battley stared at the diamonds for so long that the situation became intolerable. Yet, as if by common consent, the others did not break the silence. At last, Battley drew a deep breath, and turned away.

He began to move towards the door, Valerie thought that Webb was going to let him go, but, just as the old man reached for the handle, Webb broke his silence.

'Oh, Battley, just a moment!'

'Yes, sir?'

'You've seen the necklace before, I suppose?' Webb sounded casual, and Valerie was sure that he was deceptively so.

'I have, sir,' said Battley.

'Where?'

'In this house, sir.'

'To whom does it belong?'

'I couldn't tell you that sir,' said Battley. His voice was quite steady, although obviously he was still labouring under strong emotion. 'Time I mind it, it belonged to the first Mrs Mottram. Later, to Mrs James. 'Tis a family piece, sir. If Mr Silas was alive, it would be his. It was his to bestow on whomever he chose to bestow it, sir.'

The unaffected dignity in the old man's words was impressive. Talking seemed to ease him, and his eyes grew calmer. Webb nodded, as if satisfied, but then asked:

'Why were you so surprised to see it?'

Battley considered, and then said ruminatively:

'You ask me a question that is hard to answer, sir. I did not expect to see the diamonds here, tonight. It was said that they were lost.'

'Who said that?' asked Webb, quickly.

'If ye wish to know, sir, I'll tell 'ee – later.' Battley looked at the Inspector as if denying him to press the question, and, when Webb did not answer, turned to Valerie and asked.

'Will ye be wanting anything else now, ma'am?'

'No, Battley, thank you.'

'Then good-night, ma'am.' He bowed comprehensively to Valerie, Lynda and Webb, and went out.

Lynda was the first to move; she turned to the table, where Webb had put the tray, and poured out three cups of tea. There was a glint of mischief in her eyes as she looked at Webb.

'You've chanced on a family scandal, Inspector,' she said.

'Oh?' Webb raised his eyebrows.

'I shouldn't have told you but for Battley,' she said. 'He would have done so, sooner or later, I expect – and in any case, you'll be curious enough to dig it up somehow, and try to make more of it than there is.' She sipped her tea. 'About four or five years ago we had a little family weekend party here. It was one of Uncle Silas's rare extravagances. Just Uncle Silas, my brother William, Robin, Charles and I. Silas was very mysterious and secretive about it, and we understood that on the Sunday he was going to make a statement. I've never even guessed what it was to be about.

She paused.

'What prevented Mr Mottram from telling you?' asked Webb.

'A robbery,' said Lynda, a little too lightly. 'The safe was opened, and the necklace, together with some money, was stolen. It couldn't have been the servants – there were only two, besides Battley – who were at some function in the village. It *might* have been someone from outside, but everything pointed to its being one of the cousins.' She looked quizzically at him. 'Distressing family event, wasn't it?'

'Were the police informed?' asked Webb.

'No-o. The police weren't told.' Lynda grew brusque, giving the impression that she wished she had remained silent. 'Uncle Silas was quite convinced that one of us had stolen it. Each of us underwent a most distressing interrogation – that's the word, isn't it? – but, of course, no one admitted it. The really *funny* thing,' she added more lightly, 'was when he talked to William! William came out as red as a turkey-cock, and he went off storming within half-an-hour. The rest of us stayed until the Monday, because Silas had a heart attack after lunch on the Sunday. When he'd recovered, relations were somewhat strained. All three of us expected to hear from the police afterwards. I know Robin told him – Silas – that he was a damned fool if he didn't consult them.' She shrugged her shoulders. 'Silas said he would not have the police interfering in a private matter, that he had his own suspicions, and the affair would not be forgotten.'

Webb said thoughtfully.

'And what happened to the money? Was that ever recovered?'

'I don't think so. It wasn't much for Silas – about two hundred pounds, I think. Naturally – ' she eyed Webb steadily – 'I was the chief suspect.'

'And why?' asked Webb.

Lynda shrugged, with a show of indifference.

'I was always spending more than I could afford at the time,' she said. 'As the black sheep of the family, I was the most likely thief! I *didn't* touch the safe, of course – I didn't even know how to open it! – but there it was. William has treated me like a leper ever since.'

'And your uncle?' asked Webb.

'He behaved much the same as he'd always done,' said Lynda.

'When did you last see him?' asked Webb.

The question came so easily and quietly that it hardly seemed to have any connection with the murder. But Lynda saw what was really behind it. She laughed.

'A pretty trick, Inspector! I didn't see him on Sunday night, but I don't mind you knowing that I did see him last week, on Friday afternoon.'

'And how was he in health?'

'As well as I've ever known him,' said Lynda, 'and quite adamant, as usual. I wanted to borrow a hundred pounds, and he refused without charm or courtesy. I had made my bed, etc. etc. I didn't seriously expect to have any luck,' she added, lightly. 'I was merely taking advantage of the fact – as every true adventuress would! – that he asked me to call.'

'Why did he want to see you?' asked Webb.

Lynda raised her eyebrows.

'Mainly about Robin's impending marriage. Did I know the "young woman"? Had I any views on her? Why hadn't I told him that Robin was thinking of getting married? Was she the predatory kind, with an eye to Robin inheriting a substantial fortune? To all such questions, I answered "no". He seemed angry because Robin hadn't consulted him about the marriage, but since he never showed the slightest interest in anything any of us ever did, I couldn't agree with him that Robin had acted disloyally.'

'I'd no idea!' exclaimed Valerie.

'Darling,' said Lynda, 'I may be hard-hearted, callous, disrespectful to the dead, and all that, but it remains a fact that I had no love for Uncle Silas, and that I don't think you missed anything by not knowing him. Had he come to visit you, he would probably have made your life unbearable. He had exalted views on the status of the family, you see.'

Valerie said: 'But Robin saw him, *before* we were married. He arranged to rent The Paddocks!'

Lynda said, gently: 'Of course. Silas may have been fooling me, but I got the impression that Robin forgot to mention that he was about to get married!'

Valerie's heart sank.

It was not that she disagreed with that method of handling a difficult and querulous relation; but Robin might have told her that some kind of subterfuge had been necessary.

She was forced to remember again that Robin had been alone for those fateful three hours, in which he might have seen Uncle Silas.

Webb nodded, as if finding this peculiar family behaviour quite understandable, and asked:

'Did you quarrel with him, Miss Mottram?'

'Oddly enough, I rarely quarrel,' said Lynda airily. 'I told him that I saw he hadn't improved, but that was about all. Robin was the Big Bad Boy at the moment, so I did not get the usual lecture. *I* did not, however, kill Silas, Inspector.'

'I hope you didn't,' said Webb. He looked at his watch, and stood up. 'It's past eleven! I shouldn't have kept you so long.' He smiled at Valerie, quite friendly now. 'There's no ill-feeling, I trust? I am beginning to think that somebody is deliberately trying to make it difficult for you Mrs Fayne.'

Valerie said: 'No-o, there's no ill-feeling. But – why were you so suspicious of me?' She put only a slight emphasis on the 'were' although she had no doubt that Webb remained suspicious, and would be so until the case was settled.

Webb hesitated.

'I'm afraid I can't tell you any more at the moment, Mrs Fayne,' he said, 'but at the appropriate time I will do so. Now – what do you want me to do with the necklace?'

'Perhaps you had better take it,' suggested Valerie.

'It will come in useful as Exhibit A, B or C,' added Lynda lightly.

Chief Inspector Webb, with the box under his arm, walked alone towards the end of the drive where he had left his car. He wished earnestly that he had a reliable and intelligent 'aide'. Kennedy, whom he had seen earlier, so full of his own importance, was useless. The optimistic Bennett, while an admirable routine man, was quite void of constructive ideas. Normally, Webb was quite happy to commune with himself, but this case was different; the man from the Yard would be at Listow in the morning, and Webb wanted to have a comprehensive report for him. He pondered the wisdom of seeing whether the Chief Constable were up, but decided against it. He had better work it up himself, and hope that the Yard man would be friendly and co-operative.

He bent to unlock his car, but the key stuck. Struggling with it, the seventh sense of all good policemen warned him. But the warning came too late. He had the vaguest intimation of a man standing behind him, and no time at all to call out or defend himself, before he was struck over the head, and fell heavily to the ground.

Chapter 12

The Mortification of Webb

Webb knew that the box with the necklace had gone.

He did not know whether he had taken two minutes, or five, to recover and stand supporting himself against the car. His head ached furiously, and he could not clear his mind enough to decide, at once, if he should go back to The Paddocks and tell the two women what had happened. He was angry with himself, not to say mortified that the necklace had been taken so easily. His anger mounted, and became centred on the thief.

He decided to tell Kennedy what had happened, and to get the three men in the grounds busy on a search which, he knew, would probably be fruitless. He himself would telephone Listow and report the theft, using Carrow's telephone. Thus, the two women would not be alarmed.

Could they have had anything to do with the theft?

On the surface, the question appeared absurd. It did not seem possible that either Mrs Fayne or Miss Mottram had had time to tell an accomplice and to send him in pursuit. But it could not be entirely ruled out.

Who else, other than the one who left it outside the door, could have guessed that he would have the necklace? And would that one, after giving it up, take such a risk to get it back?

His head bandaged by Carrow's wife, Webb brooded heavily over the unexpected turn of events. Against his first convictions he was beginning to believe in Valerie Fayne's honesty. And there was the evidence of both women to testify to the fact that the anonymous note, as well as the parcel, had been slipped furtively in the porch.

If she were innocent, someone was trying to implicate her and the same unknown person was trying to scare her. These conclusions were unavoidable.

When he reached Listow, Webb wrote a brief report, and

had it sent by special messenger to Colonel Grey's house, so that Grey would know about it first thing in the morning.

He was, himself, at the office soon after half-past eight the following day, hoping to get an hour's work done before either Grey, or the man from the Yard put in an appearance. Bennett had not arrived. No reports of any significance had come in during the night. Kennedy had not even sent one of his wordy, superfluous commentaries.

Webb connected two things together in his mind – the theft of the pictures, and that of the necklace. It seemed reasonable to assume that he had only to find one man to solve both crimes.

He had been in the office for less than five minutes when Kennedy looked in, to say that Mr Robin Fayne and Lt. Commander Fayne had arrived at the house just after eight o'clock.

'Thanks,' said Webb. 'Anything else?'

'Nothing at all, sir. Just nothing.' Kennedy was effusively cheerful.

'Everyone was silent at the house last night?'

'No doubt about that, sir. I watched from the landing myself. Battley was the first to get up, about six o'clock. The two ladies were up just after seven, when Mr Fayne telephoned to say what time he would arrive. That's the lot, sir.'

'All right, thanks,' said Webb, sourly.

It was then a quarter to nine. He started to look through the files again, but had read through no more than half a page of Bennett's school-boyish writing when the telephone rang.

'Hallo,' he grunted into it. 'Webb speaking.'

'Superintendent Folly is on his way up, sir.'

'Folly?' echoed Webb. 'Folly?'

'That's right, sir.'

Webb's heart sank; for of all who could have been sent from Scotland Yard, the vain, the eccentric, the mercurial *bon vivant* Folly, was, at this moment, the one he would have chosen least. He replaced the receiver and lit a cigarette, pushing the files away from him. He was still confused, his head ached, and he knew that so far he had acquitted himself badly. His high hopes of having something promising for the Yard man to work on were dashed, he had nothing to confess but failure and crass carelessness.

There was a tap at the door, and a constable announced:

'Superintendent Folly, sir.'

'God help me!' thought Webb.

A large man entered the office, an exceedingly bulky man, swaying swiftly forward on small exquisitely shod feet.

Not only his physical bulk but his mental bulk fanned out and enveloped a humbled Webb. He remembered Folly's appetite for fame, for Boeof Stroganoff, and for results – especially for results, and the humiliating fact that none of these things was he, Webb, likely to provide.

He forced himself to look cheerful.

'Hallo, Superintendent! I'm glad to see you, but I didn't expect you just yet.'

'Dear boy, you must do something about those stairs.' A plump white hand, apparently boneless but of unexpected strength was waved before him.

'Came down on the milk train. No breakfast. Not so much as a cup of tea. Fortified, twenty-eight stairs may be tolerable, unfortified no man of full stature can be expected to face them with equanimity.'

'Twenty-seven to be exact,' said Webb stubbornly. 'We have a canteen, shall I have something brought up?'

'Twenty-eight, I repeat. A canteen you say? Excellent! I suggest, in all diffidence, a little something – the phrase is rhetorical – to be sent up here immediately.'

Giving instructions over the telephone Webb broke off to murmur combatively: 'The stairs – I've always understood –'

'Say no more, dear boy, say no more!' Folly cried generously. 'Nobody likes to be put right on their own staircase. On such an occasion one pardons, one condones irascibility. Had a bump on the head?' Folly peered forward, blinking. 'See you have, this case?'

Webb drew a deep breath, replied in the affirmative and gave the details as baldly as he could. It would be better to get it over, and accept with as good a grace as he could muster the resultant partonage and pointed humour.

Folly heard him out, then smiled. It was a smile quite unrelated to Webb's gloomy prognosis.

'Too bad! Much too bad, Webb! Had my pocket picked at Epsom in '37. Never heard the last of it. Life!' continued

Folly, the gleam fading. 'It doesn't give you a fair deal, does it?'

Webb began to feel better.

'It didn't last night,' he admitted.

'No. These diamonds – funny thing, Mottram – the *corpus* – told me about them. Said he thought whoever had stolen them had designs on his life. Admitted that he suspected one of his relations, and only his loyalty to the family prevented him from reporting it. God! What a seething amalgam of emotions that phrase covers up! But I let it go. The old boy was frightened, Webb. Convinced me he had a good reason for being scared too. That's why I let you people in on it so soon. By the way – congratulations!'

Webb looked up, astonished.

'Congratulations!' said Folly, briefly raising a flipper-like hand, as a friendly seal might salute another from a distant rock. 'Might have been a week before that body turned up. I told Mottram he ought to have reported the robbery at once, but his family arrogance was even greater than his fright. Still, he was murdered. I've been looking through the reports you telephoned through. Killed at this house – The Paddocks, isn't it? In the attic. Handle of lethal weapon sawn off while in body. Cool nerve. Interesting case. Glad you asked me to look in. Tell me if I tread unwittingly on local feelings. Tiresome things, feelings. Entangling.'

Webb laughed, in sheer relief.

'I'll let you know,' he promised.

Folly's breakfast arrived, and as he ate, delicately and with relish, Webb gave him the rest of the story, in greater detail. Folly nodded impassively, from time to time asked for clarification, but did not make any comment until his meal finished simultaneously with Webb's statement.

He nudged the tray away. 'How few, how distressingly few, possess the art of scrambling eggs! But for those blessed few it's a lost endowment, Webb, a lost endowment.

'Very complicated picture, isn't it? Old man hated like poison, one of his family suspected of theft, and all of them, except perhaps William Mottram, waiting for him to die. Well, now! We've been lucky. We've been building up the case against the family, in the hope that something would happen!' He smiled, seraphically, 'Charles Mottram. Young dare-devil. No harm in him, as far as I've been able to find out. Still, you never know. Wealthy friends, and he's not wealthy. On the contrary – lost heavily on horses, so went to the money-lenders, but, as yet, no scandal attached to his name. Good fellow, nice fellow. Like his brother, Robin.'

'I haven't met either of them,' said Webb.

'Neither have I. Details collected by my hard-working Sergeant Cross. Down with 'flu, so we'll have to do this between us.'

Webb felt the stirring of an emotion he had not experienced since he was fifteen.

'Robin Fayne, now,' continued Folly scowling ferociously. 'Steadier type than his brother, but very charming. *Very* charming. One or two interesting things developed about him. Had a devil of a row with his uncle about a year ago. No one knows what about. The servants at Mottram's house knew of it, but that's all. Robin stormed out, swearing he would never darken the door again. Reconciliation, no one knows how or why, about six months afterwards.' Folly paused. '*Per*-haps!'

Webb said:

'Robin Fayne's wife is badly worried. I might have got something out of her, but for the cousin.'

'Ah, the lovely Lynda!' Folly's expression became too bland, too innocent. Webb's contentment was suddenly clouded by the suspicion, am I being fooled? Is he telling me everything?

'Now Robin had a row with Uncle Silas and patched it up,' Folly was saying with the air of a simple story-teller. 'He may have hugged a secret hatred, and he may have wanted to get hold of his share of the Mottram pelf because of this marriage of his, and the added expense of keeping up The Paddocks. Silas fleeced him. He was also very angry because Robin hadn't told him that he was about to be married. So we've evidence that Robin's new-found affability was at least partly feigned. Let's get on to Lynda – she's got her wits about her, hasn't she?'

'She has!' said Webb, feelingly.

'Very much so,' said Folly. 'My man Cross saw her, and he came back with his code of morals severely shaken, not to say completely ruined! But I dug deep. Lynda has the reputation of being a hussy. One breach of promise that she won, another that she didn't proceed with. Vague murmurings about being cited as co-respondent in divorce actions. She doesn't give a damn for anyone, but I've a feeling – only a feeling, mind you, that it's a pose. Her maid – she had a maid until a few months ago – swears by her. No one in this world as wonderful as Lynda Mottram. So it may be. I'll get to that in a moment. Who's next?'

'William Mottram.'

Folly's infantile features puckered as if he were faced with a wholesome, but unpalatable, pudding.

'The insufferable bore! Oh, yes, I know William. A most praiseworthy barrister. Carries the juries by the sheer weight of his verbiage. Outside that, a pompous ass. Too much money. Happily married to a mild little woman who thinks he's wonderful. No family. If William killed his uncle, it wasn't for the money motive. Next?'

'The only other possibilities,' said Webb, cautiously, 'appear to be Battley, and the previous tenant at The Paddocks – a man named Dering, who left Pelham in a hurry. He had three years of his agreement to run, but he didn't stay, and Silas Mottram didn't keep him to it.'

'Oh?' said Folly, 'that's interestingly out of character. I'd like to know more about this Dering. Anything else?'

'There's one other thing,' Webb told him. 'I had an anonymous letter telling me that Mrs Fayne was not as innocent as she seemed, and that she has visited Pelham, on and off, for some time, a fact which she flatly denies. The letter on its own wouldn't have impressed me, but the village people don't often go wrong.'

'How'd you find it out?'

'I put a man on at The Angel – the village pub – for an hour or two last night. My man asked no questions but several people talked of having seen Mrs Fayne. Or,' amended Webb, quietly, 'of thinking they had.'

'Hum!' said Folly, 'interesting. Well, we'll soon have the whole bunch together, except Dering. We'll have to look for him, and find out why he ran away. That's what it amounted to. And we have the mysterious diamond-thief and canvas-snatcher to deal with. That might be one of the relatives – or someone working for one of them. Not likely one of themselves, for Charles has been in the North; Lynda certainly didn't hit you; Robin was away, and William, I know, was in London. But it isn't as pretty a picture as it seems, Webb. Nothing like as pretty! Lynda didn't let out that she's been to Pelham lately, did she?'

Webb started. 'Are you sure?'

'Oh, yes. She came down on Sunday. William did too. Probably Charles, Charles has put it around that he's been in the North and doesn't want to come South because he's liable to be recalled at any moment. Very plausible, but not true. Charles, in the North, couldn't have knifed Uncle Silas – but Charles in the South is a different matter.'

Chapter 13

Cousin William Arrives

There was no doubt, Folly said, that the relations of Uncle Silas had all been in Pelham at the week-end – or, in Charles's case, near enough to have made a hurried return trip. Webb began to appreciate more fully the fact that Scotland Yard had had a good start; had he tried to handle it on his own, he would have been in serious trouble.

He went with Folly to see Colonel Grey. While they were with the Chief Constable, a telephone message came in to say that William Mottram had arrived at The Paddocks.

'Excellent!' cried Folly, beaming benevolently on the Colonel, who rather taken aback at this usurping of a role he usually reserved for himself, accepted the benevolence a little uncertainly. 'Most excellent. I suggest that Webb and I go out and see them now that they're all together, and before William has time to put them up one or two ideas on how to sidetrack the police. Can't allow that, eh, sir? We have your permission to go at once, then? Good. Come along Webb.'

Valerie had been undecided and unhappy when Robin and Charles arrived.

She took to Charles, just as she had taken to Lynda, but for the first time, she felt some restraint with Robin. The fact that he had been downstairs when she had been in bed on the Monday evening seemed to grow out of all proportion to its importance. It was hateful to entertain the slightest doubts about Robin, but she could not dismiss them.

For one reason and another, it was nearly eleven o'clock before she was alone with him. She had gone upstairs when she heard the sitting-room door open. Then Robin's footsteps followed, quick and light.

He came into the bedroom, and as she turned to face him

he strode across the room, hugged her, and lifted her clear from the floor.

'My sweet, this is the very devil!'

She forgot her suspicions, forgot everything but the fact that this was the old Robin, *her* Robin.

He put her down, at last, though still holding her.

'At least, you're meeting the relations!' he said, a little ruefully. 'You won't take to William as you have to the others, but he's all right at heart. You've had a pretty clear picture of Uncle Silas, too. And – ' his eyes laughed at her – 'I'm in the dog house!'

'I – I feel a beast, but – ' she began.

'I didn't tell Uncle Silas about our getting married, because I didn't want to precipitate another row,' interrupted Robin. 'And I didn't tell you that I hadn't told him because – well, it's such a barbed, easily misunderstood thing to say. You might not have believed the petty and ridiculous reason – that it was solely because he hadn't been consulted.' Robin stood back, looking at her steadily. 'You know, I think there's something else on your mind.'

Valerie drew a deep breath.

'There is. Robin – you know that the police say that he was killed here, about midnight on Monday?'

'I know that they think so.'

'Well – ' she found it hard to put into words now – 'well, suppose they press you about where you were on Monday evening? Robin, I'm frightened in case they get around to that. I can't say that you were with me every moment – at least I can, but I might slip up. And I remember telling Mrs North that I had a headache on Monday evening and went to bed early. The police have been questioning her. Supposing she gives them a hint, and they follow it up?'

Robin whistled softly.

'I'd forgotten about that. A pretty bad construction could be put on it.'

'I know,' said Valerie, miserably.

Robin stared at her, his face expressionless; and then his lips began to curve. He laughed, unexpectedly, and hugged her again.

'I didn't do it!' he said, gaily. 'Cross-my-heart, sweetheart, I didn't do it! I was in the morning-room all the time, and *I* didn't see Silas.'

'Thank heavens!' exclaimed Valerie.

'So *that's* been on your mind?' said Robin. 'Well, it's a position we must face up to. If the police know that we weren't together all the time, they might suspect more than they should. I suppose it *is* possible that Uncle Silas was killed here, and it would certainly seem likely that I knew he was downstairs – I could easily have talked with him, without your knowing.'

'Are you going to tell them?'

Robin frowned, and stepped towards the window. Valerie wished that he had not evaded her gaze.

'We-ll – would it be wise? Need we tell them yet? It looks to me – ' he turned and faced her, openly enough now – 'as if we might stir up unnecessary trouble. They'll probably find out who did it before long, and we'll have caused ourselves needless worry.'

'I suppose so,' said Valerie, trying to speak brightly.

'Then that's settled.' He was relieved, there was no doubt about that. 'As for the murder – I can't believe that it was Lynda or William. Charles was up North, so he couldn't have done it. Someone else – I wonder who had a reason?'

'I suppose the police will find out,' said Valerie.

'Oh, they're bound to! The trouble is that they'll probably be damned unpleasant during the proceedings. I wish – ' he broke off, staring along the drive. 'Hallo! Visitors!'

'Who is it?'

'I suspect, Cousin William,' said Robin. 'Yes, it is.' Valerie joined him as a figure disappeared into the porch, Robin said thoughtfully:

'As he's head of the family now, he'll probably want to throw his weight about a little, I think – ' he frowned – 'it wouldn't be a bad idea if I went downstairs and helped the others to jolly him up a bit. That way he won't give you such a bad impression. Shall I?'

'Yes, you'd better,' said Valerie.

He went out, appearing not to notice her lack of enthusiasm.

She stood staring down at the departing taxi. She was afraid. It was obvious to her that Robin had something to hide. His whole manner proclaimed it. She had quite expected him to laugh at her fears and to tell the police about Monday evening. Instead, he had persuaded her that it would be risky. *But there could only be a risk if he had done something which the police must not know about.*

Why should he want to keep the truth from the police? What *had* he done in those three vital hours?

She hated herself for distrusting him, but he had shown so little faith in her. If he had some secret, surely she had a right to share it.

There had sprung an invisible barrier between them, where none had been before. It had come when he had stepped to the window, avoiding her eyes. Everything else faded beside the fact that he had not thought her worthy of his trust.

'This won't do!' she said, fiercely, 'I mustn't let myself go, there must be an explanation for everything!'

She turned abruptly to the dressing-table mirror, busied herself with her face, her hair. She wished she had time to change into a cooler frock – like the flowered one Lynda was wearing that morning – but decided against it. She looked at herself again and decided it did not matter really whether Cousin William liked her or not, and went downstairs.

From the hall, she heard a booming voice.

'I tell you, Robin, it was preposterous! Preposterous! There was no excuse at all for such secrecy. You might at least have told *me*. I cannot understand it, but I *can* understand Uncle Silas being most put out. In fact, he most certainly was.'

'Hush!' exclaimed Charles.

'My dear boy,' said William, 'surely it is safe to say what we think in *this* house? We are all closely bound by ties of blood. We *know* that Uncle Silas was angry because of Robin's hasty marriage. He assumed – and not unreasonably – that a marriage in such haste must have been prompted by circumstances which, however broadminded we might be, could only be deplored. *Was* there any need for this hurried, ill-considered match?'

Valerie coloured to the roots of her hair.

Robin spoke, in a deceptively casual voice.

'William, you have a mind as warped as Uncle Silas's was. Let it be known now, once and for all, that I married Valerie because I am in love with her, and, please God, shall remain so. I did not inform any member of the family because I knew they might – in your case almost certainly would – hand the information on to Silas.'

'And why should Silas have been kept in ignorance?'

'That,' said Robin, 'is my business.'

'Now come, Robin – '

Robin's voice grew sharper.

'We've talked enough about it. And if you say so much as one word to cause Valerie anxiety or embarrassment, I'll smash your smug face in!'

'There is no need to adopt such a bellicose attitude,' said William, stiffly. 'I merely wished to arrive at the facts.'

'You have.'

'And I must admit,' went on William, pontifically, 'that I would be grieved to think that anything I should do or say, might mar the happiness of your wife. On the contrary, as the head of the family, I shall do my best to welcome her.' The climb-down was handsome if not enthusiastic.

'Now that William has been put in his place,' said Lynda, gently, 'isn't it time we talked about something else?'

'Such as?' asked William.

'Is there anything more interesting than ourselves?' said Lynda. 'Silas was murdered, and any one of us might have killed him. As far as I can gather, some one is trying to get Valerie suspected. While I can forgive anyone killing Silas, I can't forgive that extra, rather unpleasant, touch.'

'Don't be an ass, Lyn!' said Charles, bluntly. 'How *could* it be one of us?'

'It is a preposterous suggestion,' brayed William.

'The police don't think so,' said Lynda. 'Once they find out that some of us saw Silas on Sunday, it's *almost* as good as a confession! Can you imagine it, William? Prominent barrister questioned in murder case.'

'There is no need for the police to know about our seeing Silas,' said William, quickly.

'I thought you had some commonsense,' said Charles. 'Of course they will find out, and we'll have to tell them before they learn from some other source. Otherwise we're going to get into serious trouble.'

'I absolutely forbid it!' cried William.

'Dear William,' said Lynda sweetly, 'how like you are to poor, dear King Canute.'

'Well, here's my confession for one!' said Charles. 'I came down to Pelham on Sunday to see Silas. He asked me to say nothing to anyone else about it – except Robin – I don't know what Silas told you, but I do know it must look as if I came down on the sly. The police might think I came down on Monday too. I didn't, but I'd have a heck of a job to prove where I was. *I've* no reason to be afraid of the police, but I shall have if we start trying to hide the truth.'

'There's something in that,' Robin admitted. 'I didn't see Silas, he phoned me, saying I was to say nothing to anyone about him being in the neighbourhood. He also said that he knew who had stolen the diamond necklace.'

Valerie's heart leapt; and Lynda said:

'He told me the same, when I saw him at Listow.'

'I also saw him in Listow,' said William, grudgingly. 'I considered the secrecy unnecessary, as well as unpleasant. He told me, however, that he proposed to accuse the thief face to face. He had some notion, I understood, of getting us together one day in the near future, and –'

'Gloating over it,' said Charles. 'Let's face it, that's just what he was going to do. He kept us all in suspense, so that whoever took that necklace would be bound to have a pretty rough time in the waiting period. That's *if* one of us took it.'

Lynda said, lightly:

'If I were a policeman, and I knew about all this, I would say that whoever took the necklace killed Uncle Silas to keep him quiet. Wouldn't you? And in view of that, ought we to tell them everything?'

'Believe it or not, I have a rudimentary knowledge of the law,' said William, with clumsy irony. 'I declare emphatically that if the police are told the whole truth, then they will think exactly as Lynda prophesies. It will be folly, in my opinion, to make any statement whatsoever. It will – '

'Strengthen the possibility of one of us being hanged,' said Lynda. 'Is that what you mean?'

Chapter 14

The Prodding Process

Valerie, still near the door, knew that it was exactly what William meant, despite the denials which he voiced with a great show of strong indignation.

Valerie wondered if they knew that the door was open.

Had it been shut, little could have been heard in the hall. As it was, her confusion – mostly concerned with Robin, although she had not yet forgiven William for his innuendo – was heightened when she heard a sound in the morning-room.

It was a stifled sneeze.

She stepped quickly towards the room, going in as if unaware that anyone was there. She pulled up short at the sight of a tall, heavily-built man with a quiff of fair hair, and an embarrassed smile.

'Oh!' she exclaimed, as if startled. 'What are you doing here?'

'Good-*morning*, Mrs Fayne.' Sergeant Bennett was hastily buttoning something into his pocket. A notebook, she thought mechanically. Dear Sergeant, you're not quite quick enough. 'I – er was just having a look around,' he added, brightly.

'So I see,' said Valerie, coldly. 'Is it part of the police's duty to listen at keyholes and hide behind doors?'

She frowned and stared into his face again. She had to make sure whether all that had been said in the sitting-room had been overheard. If it had, Robin and the relatives would have to tell the police themselves, and soon, before the report went through. Further deception could only bring disaster as great as could result from Robin's decision to say nothing of his opportunity for killing Uncle Silas.

She was about to ask when Webb was coming out, but at that moment she saw a car turn into the drive and she recognised it as Webb's. There were two men in it, but she could see neither of them clearly. She nodded carelessly, and as casually as she could, slipped into the sitting-room.

All four of them looked at her, Charles with a friendly smile, Lynda inquiringly, and William with an appraising air which did not wholly conceal his anxiety.

Robin's expression defied her; he was smiling lazily, but his eyes were keen.

She closed the door, and with her back to it said carefully:

'You should have made sure that you couldn't be overheard. A policeman in the morning-room has been making notes.'

'No!' exclaimed William, aghast.

Valerie eyed him dispassionately, surprised at her own coolness.

'I suppose you're William?'

'My dear!' exclaimed William. 'Of course, I – '

She had not the heart to tell him that she had heard practically the whole conversation, but she cut him short by saying:

'I think Webb's here.'

'Ah,' said Lynda. 'So we must beat his henchman to it. You get your own way, Charles, so one at least of us is content.'

'It's damned awkward,' said Robin.

Valerie turned to him, and said quietly:

'It's the only sensible thing to do. Robin, I'm *not* really one of the family, but because I'm an outsider, I can see the difficulties much more clearly than you can. It's quite useless to try to deceive Webb. Tell him everything, and then let him get on with his job. After all, the only reason to fear him would be a guilty one, wouldn't it?'

Robin was looking at her, her smile a little strained.

'Ye-es.' Then more crisply: 'Yes! That's what we'll do. Darling, I really am sorry that I didn't tell you, but – '

'We've got much more to worry about than that, now,' said Valerie, equably. She was hurt badly enough by what she knew, but a far deeper regret lay in the fact that Robin had kept something from her for fear that she would betray him. A cold, gripping, anxiety possessed her, despite the naturalness of her answer.

Not *Robin*; Robin could not have done this thing!

She saw Lynda glance towards her as William buttonholed Robin, without further remonstrances. Charles stood aside, smiling diffidently. Beside Robin, who stood over six feet, and William, nearly as tall, Charles looked stocky and over-shadowed.

He began to fill his pipe.

Someone walked towards the sitting-room – Valerie thought it was Battley. Then Frend turned into the drive, a slight wind ruffling his dark hair.

'Your parson friend,' Lynda said. 'Val – ' she gripped Valerie's arm and whispered, 'Don't give way.'

Valerie looked at her sharply.

'What do you mean?'

'I've an idea how you feel,' said Lynda. 'Robin – opportunity – trivial deceptions. But don't give way! Robin's – ' she sought for a word, and contented herself with: 'Robin's all right.'

Valerie smiled at her gratefully, wondering whether Robin had been able to read her thoughts as easily. Then Battley entered, to inform them that the Inspector had arrived with a stout stranger.

'Stout stranger?' Robin frowned. 'I wonder if they've called in the Yard?'

No one volunteered a comment. When Valerie returned from the front door after admitting Frend, Robin strode across the room to greet him.

'I've got to thank you for looking after my wife,' he said. 'I do, most sincerely.'

'It was the only thing to do, Mr Fayne, and a pleasure.'

They made an odd contrast. Both were the same height, but alike in little else, Robin's features being blunt and rugged, Frend's, pale and aquiline. There was a little desultory conversation but under it an uneasiness which no practiced observer could fail to see.

Frend was on the point of going as Webb and Folly walked through the house towards the sitting-room.

Bennett had reported the overheard conversation to them, and both were in a confident mood.

'Excellent! Mrs Fayne will have told them that they were overheard, and we'll get a nice, frank, statement from them all!' said Folly with deepening satisfaction.

'Bennett shouldn't have betrayed himself,' said Webb. striving by this criticism to keep fresh in Folly's memory the excellence of his man, rather than rend him in reproof.

'Now, now! Man's human, and sneezes have been the downfall of Kings. Time may teach Bennett to hold his nose, or disguise the explosion as a pheasant's lure cry.'

They reached the sitting-room as the door opened, and Frend and Robin appeared. All four stopped and regarded one another, Frend, looking slightly ill-at-ease.

'What, going?' Folly's face was expressionless as he regarded the vicar. 'Can you not stay for a little while, sir?'

'I reall *must* go,' said Frend, his voice unpromising.

'Must?' Folly accentuated the word, 'Hum!. Pity. Would have liked your help.'

'I don't see that I can help in any way,' said Frend, stiffly.

'You never know,' said Folly. 'Have the pleasure of seeing you later then. Good-day, sir.' Huge, unwieldy, yet not without grace, he surged through the sitting-room door.

The family, strained and apprehensive, turned to face him.

He did not smile, or employ his usual cover of flowery innuendo. Quiet, disinterested questions probed and prodded, their deadly purport hidden from the victim to the last disclosure. Of them all, Charles alone remained unruffled. It was easy to imagine him in command, imperturbable and competent. He explained his hurried trip to town and then his wire to Robin, from Liverpool, without turning a hair.

'Why did you send that wire, Commander Fayne? Why did you wish no one to know that you had been so far south? It appears to me it was a deliberate attempt to create the wrong impression.'

'That is so,' said Charles. 'Uncle Silas asked me to keep the visit secret.'

'I see. You're quite sure, Commander, that you only came south *once*? You weren't here on Monday night?'

'I was not.'

'Where were you?'

'I was travelling,' said Charles, calmly.

'Travelling,' murmured Folly. 'I *see*. You weren't at a hotel, or with friends, at the time your uncle was foully murdered. You were just – travelling! To honour your promise to your uncle. Is that the whole truth?'

'All of it,' said Charles, calmly.

'You are aware that your story cannot be checked?'

'It hadn't occurred to me that it might have to be,' said Charles.

'Commander Fayne, what part of the country did you visit on Monday night and Tuesday morning? Where did you land up after your long and tiring journey by train?'

'Liverpool,' said Charles.

'Where did you lunch?'

'At a little café not far from the docks,' said Charles.

'Are you known there?'

'I might be remembered, but I don't frequent the place.'

'No-o,' said Folly. 'No-o, I imagine that is true. Miss Mottram – ' he shot a glance towards Lynda. 'I trust that *you* will be able to find some kindly friend who knows that you were in London on Monday night.'

To Valerie's surprise, Lynda said sharply:

'Just what do you mean by that?'

'Surely the question speaks for itself,' said Folly blandly. 'Or were you *travelling*, also?'

'If you meant what I think you mean – ' Lynda, began heatedly, then added in a sullen indifference. 'I was at my flat.'

'Alone? Don't, please, misunderstand me!' Folly raised his hand, in a gesture of sophisticated tolerance. 'You have a maid at the flat?'

'I have not.'

'Dear me! So you were quite alone? Your neighbours, perhaps, looked in to see you during the evening? Between – shall we say – eight o'clock and ten o'clock? Because I would like to be reassured on that point, Miss Mottram.'

'I was in my flat – alone,' said Lynda.

'Oh. How disappointing!' mourned Folly. 'Two members of the same family with a love of solitude! Mr Mottram – ' he swung round on William. 'I wonder if *you* would mind telling me where you were on Monday evening?'

William said, portentuously:

'I was in my chambers.'

Folly's eyes widened.

'Mr Mottram, I am going to make a guess. You were in your chambers, *alone*! Your clerk was not there. You stayed there the night, because you were very busy and you wanted to start work again early on Tuesday morning. Is that not so?'

'It is perfectly true,' snapped William, angrily. 'I see no

need for you to put the words into my mouth, Superintendent. I question the propriety of your methods!'

'Come, sir!' said Folly silkily. 'You and I know each other, we know that neither of us would break those sacred rules of propriety! Did anyone come to see you at your chambers?'

'They did not.'

'Did anyone telephone you?'

'They did not.'

'Did you telephone your home?'

'I did not. My wife knew I would be there, and she could have got in touch with me, had she so desired.'

'Oh, yes. Uncorroborated statements,' accepted Folly with almost humiliating indifference. In nerve-racking silence he consulted Bennett's notebook. He nodded as if with satisfaction, and turned to face Robin.

'Now, Mr Fayne, at least you weren't travelling, or in your house alone, on Monday night!'

So it was coming, thought Valerie.

In a few seconds everything would be revealed, and any lie, detected in the telling, used against them with deadly cunning. Thank heavens, Robin had belatedly agreed that only the truth would serve.

'I was here, of course,' said Robin.

'With Mrs Fayne?'

'Yes,' said Robin, and went on quickly: 'We were both rather tired and head-achy – we'd been in the sun a lot – and we went to bed soon after the nine o'clock news.' He shot a quick smile towards Valerie, then looked back at the Superintendent, as Valerie's heart dropped in surprise and disappointment.

After surveying Robin in one of those long, uncomfortable silences, Folly turned sharply towards Valerie.

Chapter 15

More Evasions

She had to decide, on the instant, whether to lie and support Robin, or whether to tell the truth. She knew that it would have to be a lie, no matter how she hated the fact that Robin had gone back on his promise. It was the beginning of a web which would become more entangled as the hours passed.

Folly's question startled her.

'Do you sleep heavily, Mrs Fayne?'

'Why – fairly heavily, yes,' said Valerie, puzzled.

'Was your headache bad enough to make you take any drug?'

'Drug? I took a couple of aspirins, that's all.'

'And then went to sleep?'

'Why, yes, I – I didn't get to sleep immediately, but – '

'When you did drop off, did you sleep heavily?'

'That – ' she hesitated, not seeing what Folly was driving at, yet knowing there was a trap, open for her to enter. 'That's probably true,' she said, lamely.

'Come, Mrs Fayne! You know whether you slept well or badly. Did you hear anything? The sound of movement?'

'I don't remember hearing anything.'

'You have surely given that matter considerable thought,' said Folly, abruptly. 'A man was killed in this house and carried from the house into the garden, where he was buried. Either you were asleep, and heard nothing, or awake, and heard something.'

'I was asleep,' Valerie said, desperately. 'I must have been, for I heard nothing!'

'Thank you,' said Folly. His next words came lazily. 'Since you slept so heavily, you can't be sure that your husband was in the bedroom all the time?'

Valerie stared at him. Robin opened his lips, then closed them again.

'Come, come!' murmured Folly, his drooping lids lifted to reveal eyes brilliant and alert. '*Can* you be sure that he was in the room all the time? If you heard none of the noises which must have taken place, it is possible that he left the bedroom without disturbing you. I am not asking you to say that he *did*, remember. Just that he *might* have done.'

'I – I suppose so,' said Valerie, miserably.

Robin drew a deep breath. His face was very pale.

'I don't like your innuendo, Superintendent.'

Folly considered him in silence.

'Well, now! No one likes being suspected of murder! I wouldn't myself. But you're suspected. So – ' he looked blandly round the room, 'is everyone here. It doesn't necessarily mean that you committed the crime; it *might* have been done by someone outside.'

'I was praying, Superintendent, that you would at long last see that possibility,' said William, with clumsy sarcasm.

'I said "might",' pointed out Folly gently.

'As matters stand, unless this murder was committed by four people, in collusion, any *one* of you had the opportunity.' He murmured, as if to himself, '*Four* people, in collusion. All of whom dislike Uncle Silas and have a reason for wanting to get rid of him.' There was a long pause, then he added briskly. 'Well, I don't think there's any more I need do now. What do you think, Inspector?'

Before Webb could answer, Robin said stiffly:

'Are you sure that the murder was committed here?'

Despairing, Valerie watched him, realising Folly's cunning in not pressing Robin, but making it obvious that he had the opportunity, and leaving it at that.

'Oh, I think so,' said Folly, as if remembering a very small detail. 'I think so – all the evidence was in the attic.'

'Attic?' exclaimed Robin, harshly.

'Yes, that's right. You don't mind if I go and have a look up there, do you?'

'I can't stop you,' said Robin, 'but have – have you any objection to my coming with you?'

'None at all.'

There had been a moment of hesitation when Valerie expected Charles to go too. Instead, he stood by the window, smiling at some secret thought.

Upstairs Folly moved ponderously about the attic. On

a small table there was a heap of saw-dust mixed with sweepings, compiled by the industrious Kennedy. Next to it was the wooden handle of the knife which had killed Uncle Silas. Folly examined them both, then bent down, to the four little dark spots on the floor. He nodded, and stood up.

'Blood, almost certainly. Have you any idea why Mr Mottram came here, Mr Fayne?'

'I'm not sure that he did,' said Robin.

'The evidence of the murder, sir – ample evidence – is here. You have nothing to add to your statement?'

'Statement?' repeated Robin, quietly. 'I answered a question, no more than that.'

'Where were you on the Sunday evening, Mr Fayne?'

Robin looked startled. 'Why, here – no, we went out.'

'What time did Mr Mottram telephone you?'

Robin considered. 'It would be about six o'clock.'

'And then you went out?'

'Yes?'

'Not to *see* Mr Mottram, by any chance?'

'I've already told you that I didn't see him,' snapped Robin. 'My wife and I walked over the meadows and looked in at the *Angel* for a snack. Probably twenty or thirty people saw us there.'

'Splendid! It's a pity that wasn't Monday night, isn't it? So you were out for two or three hours?'

'We got back about ten o'clock,' said Robin.

'There is just one other thing. Why did you withhold the news of your marriage from Uncle Silas?'

Robin said, calmly:

'He would have disapproved.'

'For any particular reason?'

'Chiefly, because he hadn't been consulted.'

'You could have avoided that surely, by consulting him?'

'I might have done, yes,' said Robin. 'Although he would have found some other reason for making himself unpleasant.'

'Why were you so sure that he would have disliked Mrs Fayne?' asked Folly, softly.

'There was a pretty sound chance,' said Robin, dryly.

'But surely you have stronger grounds than that for believing that there would be antagonism on his part?'

'I don't see that this affects his murder,' said Robin. 'But

I didn't want to provoke a quarrel and risk going directly against him.'

'Why?' Folly's voice had the maddening insistence of a dripping tap.

Robin said, slowly:

'I have always understood that I should benefit from his will by twenty or thirty thousand pounds. Had I gone against his specific advice, he might have cut me out.'

'Ye-es,' said Folly. 'I quite understand that. But surely a secret marriage – one might almost call it an elopement – was likely to provoke him to even greater anger?'

Robin said carefully:

'You didn't know my uncle, Superintendent. He would have been angry, of course, but faced with a *fait accompli*, I thought he would have accepted it.'

'Ah. I don't doubt you knew what you were about, Mr Fayne. Seeing how matters stood, however, wouldn't it have been more natural had you told Mrs Fayne – either before or after your marriage – of this decision?'

Robin considered him evenly.

'I didn't see the need for it nor would there have been any need had this not happened. Why should she be worried by family hostility? It made no difference at all to either Valerie or me so far as our marriage was concerned. I thought it would be much better to win my uncle round, and thus make things happier. It misfired.' He shrugged.

Folly looked carefully at the ceiling. 'Just one other little thing, Mr Fayne. Your uncle did not know Mrs Fayne?'

Robin looked startled.

'Good heavens, no!'

'You're sure?'

'Of course I'm sure.'

'I just wondered if there could be any other reason for your assumption of his animosity,' said Folly, innocently. 'I suppose, she couldn't have kept anything from *you*, Mr Fayne?'

'What the devil do you mean?' demanded Robin, roughly.

'Could she have known him?' murmured Folly.

'I've told you she did not!'

'She could hardly speak for you, could she?' said Folly. 'I wonder if you can speak for her? Did she know this district before you brought her here?'

'She had never been here in her life.'

'But you have only her word for that, haven't you?' suggested Folly, softly.

Robin glared at him,

'You'll go too far, damn you!'

'No,' said Folly. 'No, Mr Fayne – only far enough to see a murderer brought to justice. That is all.'

Chapter 16

Where is Mr. Dering?

Half-an-hour later, Webb drove Folly from The Paddocks, leaving a confused and troubled party at the house. Webb's admiration for the man from Scotland Yard had increased enormously in the past few hours, but an oblique glance in his direction showed no conqueror swelled in justifiable pride. Triumph, Webb noted philosophically, was not always a golden nectar to the conqueror, and to some would always hold a touch of bitterness.

When they were out of the drive, he said:

'Are you satisfied?'

'Are you?' came from Folly's slumped figure.

Webb smiled. 'I felt like a fourth form boy taking lessons from a master!'

'Oh, nonsense!' said Folly peevishly. 'As a matter of fact, I wondered if I took rather too much on myself – after all, it's your case. You'll probably get there before I do anyway. I always see too many trees, too many paths, and Folly prancing down all of them as the Holy Avenger. There are moments,' cried Folly in an anguished voice, 'when pity wrings my heart!' He blew his nose with an enormous handkerchief, trumpeting as loudly as a wounded elephant.

Webb kept his eyes sternly on the road. Well, well! he thought, live and learn.

'As I was saying,' Folly said severely and inaccurately. 'Fayne's put himself in a tricky position, still, if he's not the man his wife thinks he is, better find out sooner than later. What do you make of them all?'

'They're all fairly true to type, I should say.'

'Ye-es. Well Charles, now. And Lynda. Surprisingly deep, both of them. I wonder if they've been up to anything together? I wouldn't put it past them. William's not at all happy – something's troubling him. One peculiar advantage that we have, Webb! The ghost of the old crime is troubling them. Good thing for us, if it makes them touchy. The murder itself might be attributed to outsiders, but not *both* crimes. Quite an unhappy family party, I should think.' He spoke, removed, remote now, as if he were dissecting a colony of ants. 'Lynda Mottram jumped on me, didn't she?'

Webb smiled.

'You were pretty broad!'

'And I meant to be,' said Folly, complacency, like a rubber ball held too long below the surface of the sea, bursting upward with gay exuberance.

'Do you know the vicar well?'

'You're not suspecting Frend, surely?' said Webb, incredulously.

'I'm suspecting 'em all!' Folly assured him, blandly. 'Even Battley, the trusted retainer. I'll have to see 'em both this afternoon, but there are one or two things to be done first. Also – that tenant fellow who hooked it. Dering, isn't it? I wonder if there'll be any news of him?'

'We could know more about him, to advantage,' said Webb.

Folly looked thoughtful.

'Ye-es,' he said, slowly. 'Much more about him – I'll tell you what, Webb, we'll have a word with the vicar and find out whether he knows the Derings and the gardener.'

'He will greet us with unflagging courtesy,' grumbled Webb, 'and courtesy of the unflagging kind is about as pregnable as a coat of mail.'

'There are chinks,' advised Folly encouragingly.

But in fact there were few. Tactfully interrogated, Frend acknowledged he had found Battley to be an admirable fellow, Silas rather less so. His mutual interests with Dering were admitted as rare flowers, pictures, and the re-covering of the church hassocks.

'Chinks!' quoted Webb bitterly, as they trudged away from the vicarage. 'What did I tell you?'

Back in Webb's office they were greeted by a grinning and jubilant Bennett, delighted to be the reporter of further evidence from Scotland Yard.

'First of all, about Miss Lynda,' he exclaimed, excitedly ignoring his notes. 'She's badly in need of ready money.

There's a firm dunning her for a bill three years old, a bill for a hundred and forty pounds for a fur coat, and a further bill for a hundred and three pounds four shillings and elevenpence for dresses supplied two years ago.

'Mr Charles Fayne, too, is heavily in debt, and resorted to money lenders. Horses,' snorted Bennett, his Methodist disapproval of owing money overborne by the manly cachet he considered 'horses' conferred.

There was nothing on William Mottram, and nothing to indicate that Robin Fayne and his wife had known each other for longer than they both declared; nor was there anything to show that Valerie had ever been to Pelham before her engagement.

'And Sir Percy Feldmann?' inquired Folly sweetly.

Retribution for so blythly ignoring his notes descended crushingly on Bennett, for it appeared that Sir Percy, lately engaged to represent the family, was considered by Folly to be the flower of the entire evidence.

Having remembered too late the imminence of his arrival, Bennett withdraw, his optimism dashed, though by no means submerged.

Webb crossed his legs, and lit a cigarette.

'So Lynda and Charles have got their motives strengthened,' he said, 'and there's no alibi for them, or – '

'Or for William!' said Folly. 'Peculiar individual, that man. He's sent for Feldmann, one of the best men he could send for. Why – what's your guess?'

'He could be scared,' said Webb, cautiously.

'Oh, he is, dear boy, he is,' said Folly. 'I knew that from the moment I heard he was in favour of covering up the story of the family skeleton. But we've a clever mind in this, Webb. Clever, adaptable sort of mind, deliberately spreading confusion. William might be trying to make us concentrate on him, in order to – '

Webb exclaimed: 'Distract attention from one of the others?'

'It could be that,' admitted Folly thoughtfully. 'Silas Mottram kept silent for years about the loss of that necklace, all for the sake of the family, and William might carry on the same tradition. However, jumping to conclusions – bad habit.'

'What conclusions?' asked Webb.

'That William knows who has done it,' said Folly. 'One thing's certain, he's taking it seriously, or he wouldn't have sent for Feldmann. Do you know him?'

'No. I've heard of him, of course.'

'Good fellow, sound fellow,' declared Folly, with the determined and emphatic air of one who gives praise where praise is not entirely due. 'We shall have to pull our socks up. Anything else troubling you, Webb?'

'Everything's worrying me,' said Webb, with a shrug. 'In particular, why did Silas Mottram cancel his appointment with Feldmann?'

'Silas didn't cancel it, he just didn't turn up. Two curious facts, emerge here. First, why did Silas arrange for an appointment on the Sunday evening? And second, why, at his summons, did *all* his relations turn up? Charles, Lynda, Robin – yes, they had reason to, although if Robin tells the truth, he didn't. But why William?'

Webb said nothing.

'If the motive were money from the old boy's estate, William knows nothing about the murder,' said Folly, then corrected himself hurriedly. 'Silly thing to say! I mean, he didn't do the murder, on that motive. But there was something powerful enough to make him come down to Listow to see Silas. Do you know what, Webb?'

'What?' asked Webb.

'The old curmudgeon had 'em all on a piece of string,' declared Folly. 'Oh, yes, he did! None of them are the type that could be easily dominated, but they jumped when he cracked the whip – including William. So far, we know that the mystery of the necklace could explain the nervousness, but William wouldn't have stolen that necklace for the money he could get for it.'

'Was it stolen for money?' asked Webb. 'If so, why wasn't it sold?'

'Good question – I'd forgotten that. I can't answer it. If we knew the whole story about the necklace, we'd be a lot better off. Now, there's one other very curious thing, Dering's disappearance, and no sign or sound of him since he left The Paddocks three weeks ago, when he booked two tickets to London for himself and his gardener – what was his gardener's name?'

'Chesterton,' said Webb.

Folly raised his eyebrows.

'Chesterton was it? It is asking much of me to believe in the authenticity of a gardener with the name of Chesterton. This unbelievable Chesterton, then, travelled with Dering, presumably to London. Since then – nothing! No hotel booking that we've been able to trace. He didn't go to any of his clubs. We've no record of a flat. The mysterious disappearance of Mr Jonathan Dering! I wonder – ' the enthusiasm drained out of his face, his body sagged. Grievances rose in him. 'Am I to hunt criminals, absconding murderers, purloiners of diamonds, on an empty stomach?' he demanded plaintively. 'There comes a time – '

'I've arranged for you to come round to my place for lunch, if you care to,' said Webb soothingly, 'my wife will be delighted.'

'In that case – ' Folly rose on tottering, but surprisingly agile feet, 'I will leave to Bennett, a younger, slimmer, easier man to sustain at longer intervals than myself, the job of fixing an appointment with Crow the picture dealer, and hasten to take advantage of your good wife's kindly hospitality. I am a simple man to feed, a small helping of Soufflé de Homard, a taste of Fricassee de Poulet, a soupcon of Camembert – '

Though used by now to Folly's rhetorical expressions and rhapsodical description of food, Webb led the way a little nervously. His fears however, proved unnecessary. Between Folly and Mrs Webb a bond, an affinity, was immediately established. 'Ah, Irish Stew!' murmured Folly reverently. 'Of all unsung gastronomic blessings, I consider the carrot to be the most magnificent, the most maligned and misunderstood of vegetables.'

Webb, both gratified and a little jealous at the joy and appreciation which radiated from Mrs Webb's countenance, and the almost identical joy and appreciation which radiated from Folly's, was relieved when at last, at half-past two, he was able to lead the way into a small shop, the facia board of which read:

A. B. Carter – Cabinet-Maker

The Superintendent, suave, replete, drew two envelopes from his pocket.

From the first, he took the handle of the knife.

'There's just a little matter we'd like your advice on, Mr Carter,' he murmured flatteringly. 'We amateurs can only make rough guesses! What's that made of?' He let Carter have the handle – which had been tested for prints without success.

'Mahogany,' said Carter, after a longer inspection than Webb thought necessary.

'Ah, I *thought* so,' said Folly. 'And what about this?'

From the second envelope he poured a little stream of sawdust. Carter peered at it, then put his nose to it and sniffed. Not satisfied, he took up a magnifying glass through which he examined the grains closely.

He looked up at last.

'Oak,' he said.

Webb exclaimed: *'What?'*

'Oak,' repeated Carter. 'It had a lot of oil and varnish on it. making it look darker. See?' He indicated one or two grains. 'Old wood, I think you'll find, and heavily polished. Too much varnish, too. Sunk right into it. But it's oak.'

'*Not* mahogany?' asked Webb increduously.

'It never *could* have been mahogany,' said Carter, disdainfully. 'It might have been a bit of very old cherry wood, or even walnut, but it couldn't have been mahogany.'

'Well, I'm damned!' exclaimed Webb. 'But you see –'

Folly prodded him in the ribs, and then picked up the handle again.

'Mr Carter,' he said, humbly. 'I don't like worrying you like this, but what kind of saw was used to get that handle off? Could you tell for certain?'

Carter peered at it through his glass, and grunted. 'All right if I saw a small piece off, hey?'

Webb watched him, while absorbing the fact that the sawdust which Kennedy had found in such triumph was of a different wood from the handle, a fact which wrecked his most convincing theory. He had built everything on the fact that Silas Mottram had been killed in the attic. Now there was no certainty about it; it was not disproved, but as evidence it was useless for a jury.

Carter went into the workshop, and returned with a hacksaw fitted with a small blade. He sawed off about half-aninch of the handle, shook his head, fitted the half-inch piece into a small vice, and, without speaking fitted another blade to the hacksaw. He took off an eighth of an inch more, scrutinised it again, and then took off a third piece, using a different blade.

'Hey!' he exclaimed. 'That's it! Same markings. Same cut. See?'

There was no doubt at all that it had been cut with a similar blade; under the glass, the markings were quite clear – and the markings of the first two pieces were much coarser.

'A size 3 blade,' said Carter. 'Is that what you want?'

'Exactly,' said Folly. 'Exactly. It *couldn't* have been done with this, could it?'

He held up the kitchen saw which Kennedy had discovered.

'No,' said Carter, emphatically. 'Far too big.'

'And what about the sawdust in the cuts?' asked Folly.

Carter peered at it, but did not take long to decide.

'Oak,' he declared. 'The same as the other in my opinion.'

'You couldn't swear to it?'

Carter looked at Folly sharply.

'Not to that. There is no doubt at all about the other. Are you going to have me in the witness box, hey?'

'Any objection, if it becomes necessary?' asked Folly.

'I always object to anything that takes me away from my work,' said Carter. 'But I can swear to one being oak and the other mahogany, and the kind of saw that was used – that's all. I can't swear to anything else.'

They thanked him, and left the little shop soon after three o'clock. Webb said nothing – he still felt shocked at the discovery, and angry with himself because he had taken so much for granted.

Folly shrugged his shoulders. 'What would you have? Good luck *all* the way?' He spread his hands in what he considered to be a Gallic gesture in tune with philosophy. 'It would be too easy. One would become bored. Now where's this fellow Crow the picture dealer.'

Crow turned out to be an old man very different in type from the cabinet-maker. Portly and genial he came forward at once from the back of a shop stacked with frames and canvases.

'It's a great pleasure to help the police, a great pleasure! And what can I do for you, gentlemen?' He beamed broadly.

Folly said:

'Have you a very large local clientele, Mr Crow?'

'Well now – I've a *good* one,' said Crow, rubbing his hands together. 'Very good investment these days you know, these oil-paintings.'

'Hum, yes,' said Folly, eyeing without favour a still-life group of a kipper, a half-gnawed apple, and what looked like a moth-eaten sealskin cap. 'Do you buy much locally?'

'Not a great deal,' said Crow. 'I travel widely in my search for good pictures, and have very good friends in other towns – London, particularly.'

'Did Silas Mottram ever visit you?'

Crow smiled. 'Occasionally, gentlemen! A *very* good judge of pictures, Mr Mottram, *very* good!'

'To buy or sell?'

'Oh, these things work both ways, you know,' said Crow. 'I have perhaps, sold more to him than he has sold to me, but then he is a collector – and a very shrewd one, I must say that.'

'When did you last see him?' asked Folly.

'Let me see, now. A month ago, perhaps. I could look in the register – I bought several little pieces from him – a Dutch seascape, by Van Wyck, a most charming piece. And a Webster. There were several others, but they were not so good.'

'And have you any of them with you?' asked Folly.

'There are bound to be some,' said Crow. He went to the back of the shop, and came back with a ledger, flipping the pages over. 'Let me see, now – April 10th, April 11th – ah! April 19th. A little less than a month ago, you see. The Van Wyck – a trifle, but undoubtedly genuine – the Webster – they've both gone. Two by unknown artists, a suspect Turner – *very* suspect – it is with the restorers at the moment. I didn't buy that from him, I wouldn't decide until the restorers had finished with it. The others are negligible. I can show you them if you wish.'

'In a minute,' said Folly, his voice becoming slower and his phrasing more laconic as his interest quickened. 'Who bought the Van Wyck and the Websters?'

'A Mr Dering,' said Crow, without hesitation. 'Mr Jonathan Dering, from The Paddocks. *Another* good judge, gentlemen, a man whose views I greatly respect. It is rather odd. He wrote to tell me that he would be calling again on Saturday – I had advised him that I had one or two pictures which would probably interest him. He is usually a very punctual and reliable gentleman but on the Saturday he said he would be arriving, he did not come.'

Chapter 17

Dealers in Pictures

'Where did Mr Dering write from?' asked Folly carefully, 'The Paddocks?'

'No, from London, I believe,' said Crow. 'I have his letter here, yes. There. You see. Just the word "London" and Thursday's date. A brief note as he was quite sure that he would be able to get here. Between ourselves, gentlemen, I was very sorry that he left the district. I did a great deal of business with Mr Dering. But customers don't leave a reliable dealer, you know. My overheads are small, and I can sell much more advantageously than many of the big London stores. Yes, indeed!'

'Where did you write to Mr Dering?' asked Folly.

'Oh – at The Paddocks. It was over three weeks ago. I had no idea that he contemplated leaving – in fact, I only heard that he had gone from Mr Frend.'

'Frend?' Webb spoke sharply. 'The Vicar of Pelham?'

'That's right. He is also a customer of mine, and a fair judge of pictures. Not – and he would be the first to acknowledge it – so good as either Mr Dering or Mr Mottram, but sound, all the same.'

'Does Mr Frend often buy pictures?'

'Only very occasionally,' said Crow, 'but he likes to look at my new ones, and he is always welcome here.'

'A very good fellow, I'm told,' cut in Folly smoothly, as if to drive from the dealer's mind any fears that they were not well-disposed towards Mr Frend. 'You say you wrote to Dering, at The Paddocks about three weeks ago, telling him you had some pictures that he might like to look at, yet nearly three weeks passed before you heard from him. What if you had sold the pictures?'

'Sold them?' Crow looked horrified. 'But I had offered them to Mr Dering!'

'He took a long time answering,' said Folly dryly.

'My dear sir, three weeks is no *time*! I have reserved pictures for particular customers for over six months! It is not always convenient for them to come at once.'

'That means you tie your money up for a tidy while,' objected Folly, practically.

'It is more than a matter of mere *money*,' said Crow, with the contempt of an artist, or an exceedingly clever business man. 'After all, one must keep faith. Mr Mottram had a fondness for the Gainsborough period, as well as the nineteenth century English school, and if I get something that I think might interest him, then he has the first choice, no matter how long he may be coming. Mr Dering's preference is for the Dutch and Italian schools. The same ruling applies to him. I should not dream of disposing of a Van Wyck, for instance, unless Mr Dering had refused it.'

'Does he often refuse?'

'Sometimes, naturally.' Crow launched into an account of the differences between some pictures of the same schools, and how the layman could see little difference but the expert a great deal; how one artist would please a collector who specialised in a certain style or period; how another, of the same school, would leave him cold. Webb listened attentively, taking his cue from Folly, whose interest was based solely on the possibility that some clue to the murder, however vague or partially submerged, might, for an instant, show itself.

They saw the pictures which Mottram had sold to Crow, and learnt how canvasses were cleaned. They were initiated into the mysteries of re-touching, of fakes and of the elementary mistakes which amateurs made when trying to identify artists. Crow blossomed out, as a man devoted to his calling.

Webb thought of Dering, Mottram and Frend visiting this place and therefore having a common interest; he thought, also, of the canvases which had been cut from their frames at The Paddocks. Hitherto he had put this down as the means of hindering identification. He had not considered the possibility of their being valuable enough to provide a motive for murder.

Folly turned the conversation to portraiture.

Crow waxed eloquent as ever. There were some portrait painters whose work would sell readily, anywhere, at any time. But the great majority of portraits had less intrinsic than sentimental value.

'Were Dering or Mottram interested in them?' asked Folly.

'Mr Mottram was, certainly,' said Crow. 'He had some really fine portraits. Mr Dering was much less interested, but I have known him buy them from time to time.'

'For re-sale, do you think?'

'He may have bought for friends and acquaintances,' said Crow. 'But what happens to the pictures before or after I get them hardly concerns me, and I do not make any conditions, of course.'

'Would you call either Mr Mottram or Mr Dering *dealers* in old masters?' asked Folly, bluntly.

Crow pursed his lips.

'Hardly,' he said, at last. 'On the other hand, they did buy and sell. You might, by stretching the term, call them dealers. I prefer to consider them as collectors and connoisseurs.'

'You know of Mr Mottram's death, Mr Crow?' asked Folly innocently.

'Indeed I do, although I had forgotten it in my enthusiasm. A most unhappy business,' said Crow, 'I feel that I have lost an old friend.'

'Did any of his relatives come here?'

'I can't be sure of that,' said Crow, after some thought. 'Oh! Mr William Mottram did, on occasions, but I cannot be sure about the others.'

'Well, that's all I need to worry you about now, Mr Crow. Thank you for your help, and for your interesting and valuable instruction. Fascinating business.'

With studied charm Folly bowed and turned away.

'Curious!' he murmured softly.

'What is?' asked Webb.

'His verbosity,' said Folly. 'Very curious indeed. He hardly referred to Mottram as a dead man, did he? No grief before I mentioned the subject. It might have been because he forgot in his enthusiasm, or it might have been because he thought it wiser not to say that he knew.'

'Now what's on your mind?' asked Webb, a little glumly.

Folly shot him a quick, bird-like glance.

'Dear boy, there's a big traffic in stolen pictures and fakes, there being plenty of fools with money. Dealers like Crow, are well-placed as go-betweens. No questions asked, payment often made in cash. Mind you, Crow might be quite straight. On the other hand, he was *very* talkative!'

'He certainly went on and on,' admitted Webb feelingly.

'Hum, yes. He may have put through one or two deals and be aware that they might lead to trouble if we pry too closely. However, I want to see that register of his, and I want his place watched. He probably knows every man on your staff, doesn't he?'

'Probably,' Webb admitted. 'What's your interest in the place?'

Folly lowered his lids and looked very sly.

'Come! Mysterious Mr Dering hasn't turned up, but pictures of value and appeal to him are being kept for his approval. If pictures are in your blood, they become as obsessional as a love of jewels. How would you like to stop being a policeman?' He lowered his voice dramatically staring at Webb through sad, vision-haunted eyes, seeing himself an outcast, a Cain among men. 'You just can't imagine it, can you? But supposing you were thrown out of the force for some misdemeanour? What would you feel like?' He answered for himself, not for Webb, the words throbbing with intensity. 'Getting back, somehow, anyhow! You'd haunt all the old places. You'd follow cases in the press. You'd cadge information and details from your friends. Hum, yes! That's what you'd do, because it's in your blood. Pictures may be in Dering's. If they are, he'll come back. *If* he's alive.'

Webb said, slowly: 'It's a remarkable parallel to Silas's disappearance, isn't it?'

'Remarkable's the word! Well, now, can you get a man from another town to come here?'

'We might get someone from Melborough. It depends on whether they have a good man to spare just now.'

Webb picked up the telephone, and in a few moments was speaking to the Melborough superintendent, who was helpful and encouraging; he had a sergeant named Unwin, whom he would send. He supposed that it was the Mottram case and commiserated with Webb on having to bear with Scotland Yard. Folly waited sardonically, knowing, as if he heard every word, how the conversation would go. Webb put down the receiver rather sheepishly. 'That's that.' His mind swung back to his own disappointment.

'Two hours ago, I had what seemed to be a case,' he said. 'Now –'

'We've two possible cases,' said Folly. 'We haven't done anything to upset your idea, we've simply created another.'

'I haven't had much to do with it,' said Webb, his voice stiff with shattered pride.

Folly said casually, cunningly, 'You're worried because the sawdust didn't come from that handle, so there's less evidence that Mottram was killed in that attic. You needn't be. We've agreed before – there's a clever directing intelligence behind all this.'

'Ye-es,' admitted Webb, slowly. His eyes kindling as they looked into Folly's enigmatic face, wreathed now in the expression best suited to salve a shaken confidence. 'The wrong sawdust might have been put there to confuse us. Is that what you're thinking?'

Folly nodded with the correct amount of emphasis. 'Also, it might have nothing to do with the case at all. From that swollen-headed Kennedy's report, it seems that sawdust was all over the floor. Well, lots of odd jobs can be done in attics. Dering was a dealer in pictures, remember, and frames are often made of oak.'

'That's right enough,' conceded Webb.

'Good! Mottram was a dealer in pictures, too.'

'Is "dealer" justified?'

'Both of them bought and sold pictures,' said Folly. 'Dealing is what it amounted to. So we have a line between Dering and Mottram. It might not lead anywhere useful, but it might equally well take us places. We can only wait and see – and do a bit more spade work while we're waiting! I'm anxious to know why Dering walked out of The Paddocks. Bet you half-a-dollar it was with Silas Mottram's concurrence.'

Webb looked puzzled. 'Why should he agree to that?'

'Well, now, dear boy, let's think over what we really *know*, Dering left the house in a mighty hurry. Robin Fayne wanted the house and got it in a mighty hurry. Curious facts, which might well be linked. Silas allowed his nephew to have a lease. So – '

'Great Scott!' exclaimed Webb. 'He wouldn't have let it if he hadn't known that Dering had broken the lease.'

'There you are, you see,' sighed Folly, exhausted at so much play of exemplary patience. 'It's as plain as a policeman's helmet! Yes, my boy, Silas knew Dering would never go back to the house. But what else is there? Go on, it's your turn.'

Webb hardly heard him.

'Silas Mottram was notoriously tight-fisted,' he said, excitedly, 'and he wouldn't release a man from his contract without a good reason. He – '

'Exactly, exactly!' interrupted Folly, still painstaking, but champing for the end of it. 'Silas was a man who exacted his due. But not only did he let Dering withhold it, he made no attempt to go after him for it. Another remarkable thing is. that Dering's only been away three weeks. The only evidence that he had gone for good was that he took his gardener, the improbably named Chesterton, away with him. Lots of people go away for a few weeks, Dering could conceivably have gone to a furnished house with a garden. But oh, no! Silas knew better than that!'

'Sound reasoning,' Webb said warmly.

'Lot's of things *appear* sound, though supported on very groggy legs,' suggested Folly with the cautious realism of one gradually opening a window on a practically recovered invalid. 'For what, indeed, do we *know* about Dering? Precious little. He dabbled or dealt in pictures. He dabbled in exotic horticulture. He had The Paddocks on a long lease and then he left it with dramatic haste and secrecy. That's about the lot.'

'He wrote to Crow from London,' Webb said.

'Oh, no!' exclaimed Folly, sharply. 'Oh, no, we can't accept that as a fact. The only fact being that Crow showed us a note which Dering is supposed to have written – we aren't even sure that it was Dering's handwriting. We didn't see the envelope. Nothing sinister in that, few people keep envelopes except for jotting down telephone numbers, or messages to the sweep. We might look for it at Crow's when we get a chance of going there.' He fell silent for a minute, then gave a fretful sigh. 'I'd give a fortune to look through Crow's place this very minute! What was I saying?'

'You were – ' Webb began.

'Ah yes,' cried Folly, impatient at Webb's plodding reiteration, agog to tackle the new, the untried. 'Let us assume that Dering *did* go to London, after making a moonlight flit from The Paddocks. All the evidence shows that he wanted to make himself scarce, but in spite of that he couldn't resist writing to Crow about those paintings. It could be because there was something very particular about them. So, Dering wants them. Someone stole certain others from The Paddocks. Paintings take a high priority, don't they?'

'They certainly do,' agree Webb.

'Deuced fascinating subject. Enormous sums of money constantly changing hands in a world full of mugs.' Folly paused in delight, to view this magnificent spectacle. 'What would I not give to search Crow's premises,' he added piously.

'Well, why don't we?' asked Webb.

Folly stared at him, then his great bulk rose, majestic as a basking whale rearing from the ocean.

'Webb! My dear, dear Webb! As you so simply say, why don't we? – Humbled I stand. I speak rhetorically of course – remembering those hitherto neglected words: "Fools wander where angels fear to tread". How necessary, how blessedly necessary, are those wanderings. I see now, prepared as I am to profit by them. What are we waiting for?'

Webb's pleasure in Folly's pleasure had a little overlaid the finer details of the speech, but he was prepared, in the interest of his continued satisfaction, to let it go at that.

As they left the police station, the necessary arrangements made. Webb said:

'There is one other thing.'

Folly looked at him sceptically, unprepared to believe in the probability of *two* rabbits being produced out of the same hat.

'I was thinking of Frend,' Webb explained. 'He might conceivably be in it, as you suggested, since he's a customer of Crow. Ought someone to keep an eye on him?'

Folly frowned portentously.

'He's the outside chance. We'll leave him until after we've seen Crow.'

They were drawing near the shop as Webb spoke again.

'Then there's another curious possibility –'

'What's that?' Folly stepped heavily off the kerb, in the direct line of an oncoming cyclist. Was there to be an attempt at yet a *third* rabbit?

'Robin Fayne,' said Webb thoughtfully, when Folly had reduced the cyclist to bewildered apology. 'We've agreed that Mottram knew The Paddocks would be available, but how did Fayne know that it might be empty? He knew that it was let to Dering, but he must have had some reason for thinking that he might be able to get it.'

Folly shot him a quick sideways glance.

He waved an airy hand. 'Oh, Silas Mottram might have told him. But let's forget that, dear boy. One thing at a time.' They drew near Crow's shop, and Folly was the first to touch the handle. 'Wasn't the door open the last time we got here?'

'Yes, it –' Webb broke off, for Folly said sharply:

'Dam' thing's locked. *Now* what's Crow up to?'

Webb suggested that the dealer might be having tea, but he spoke without conviction. Something in Folly's manner infected him with a greater sense of urgency. Folly rattled the door, banged on the plate glass and pressed the bell. Nothing happened. Turning swiftly he snapped:

'Where's the back entrance?'

'Along the street and down the first alleyway,' Webb said. 'Why, what –'

'Wake up, man!' exclaimed Folly. 'If Crow's got a guilty conscience, he might have evidence that wants destroying. Can't be sure, but it's a chance. You go the back way, I'll stay here.'

Webb hurried off. As he ran, he thought of Folly's quick suspicion. There might be no reason to suspect Crow of any part in the murder of Mottram but Folly's saw every possibility with bewildering clarity. *If* Crow were implicated, their visit must have jolted him severely. If the murder were connected with pictures, then Crow was an obvious suspect.

He raced along a narrow, stone-paved alley.

To get to the back of Crow's shop, he had to turn left into another alley, which cut through to a main road, two hundred yards away.

At the far end, a man was walking hurriedly.

There was something familiar about the way the man walked. He turned into the main road, and glanced over his shoulder, enabling Webb to catch a glance of his face.

It was Fayne!

There was the chance that he himself had been recognised, but Webb resisted the temptation to follow Robin. He reached the small garden at the back of Crow's shop and opened the gate.

The back door was standing ajar.

Haunted by Fayne's nearness, Webb pushed it open. There was no proof that Fayne had been in the shop, but there were good grounds for thinking so. A connection between Fayne and the picture dealer might help to settle a number of questions. It was possible that Fayne arrived immediately after he and Folly had left, and that Crow had locked the front door to make sure that the policemen could not take them by surprise if they returned.

He stepped into a little kitchen, which smelt of stale food, and had the untidy look of a bachelor's apartment.

Webb went forward slowly, his senses alert. There was a door leading to the shop, and another open on the right of the passage. With a startled certainty he caught a glimpse of a man's feet, the toes pointed upwards. He saw that a man was stretched out on the floor, and as he drew nearer he saw that it was Crow.

Chapter 18

Robin Goes to Listow

Valerie Fayne had stayed at The Paddocks all day.

In spite of warm friendliness on the part of Lynda, and to a lesser degree of Charles, she could not feel that she was one of the family. Robin seemed still further estranged from her. She could not overlook his deliberate attempt to deceive the police. He himself was worried, she knew, and undoubtedly he had good reason for anxiety, for he was the only one, so far as was yet known, who had had the opportunity of killing Silas.

If he knew nothing of the murder, why had he behaved so?

Lunch over, Robin and Charles stayed talking in the dining-room. Valerie supposed that it was natural that they should have much to talk about. Yet why always alone?

Lynda slipped upstairs, and following her soon after, Valerie saw William disappearing into Lynda's room. There was something secretive and crafty in his movements as he closed the door.

Valerie hesitated, and then, deliberately tip-toed into the dressing-room next to Lynda's bedroom.

Pressing her ear to the inner wall of a cupboard she heard nothing at first but a subdued murmur; then one sentence came clearly:

'No Will, I don't think anyone has the faintest idea.' And William's answer: 'I should hope not.'

Valerie slipped across to her own room, troubled by what had been said. Presently she heard William come out and the door close.

Preoccupied, still worried by these signs of intrigue she heard a man's footsteps and a tuneful whistling; it was Charles. He stopped and tapped on a door nearby. She heard him say:

'Can you spare a poor fellow five minutes?'

And Lynda's voice as a door opened softly: 'I wondered how long you'd be.'

So she had expected visits from both men.

Striving to work out a sensible solution Valerie wished she could discuss the whole thing with Robin. The others could be forgiven for not confiding in her, but Robin should have kept nothing back. She was almost sure that he was avoiding her, and a growing sense of grievance was only held in check by the underlying fear for him which harassed her all the time.

She was busying herself in the kitchen, when Joe Parker brought the promised 'gent's' bicycle. Robin, ill at ease, brightly acting the part of a carefree young husband, arrived soon after.

He inspected the machine, which was the same type as Valerie's, and paid in notes for both. Before Parker went off, Robin asked him whether he had a taxi for hire.

'I might want to go into Listow,' Robin said.

Parker's face set in gentle, obstinate lines.

'Ar,' he said. 'Outside o' my radius, that be. But I could take 'ee to the station, for the two-thirty train.'

'Is there time for that?'

'Oh, ar. I'll come right up for ye,' said Parker.

'Good!' said Robin. He spent ten minutes looking at the bicycle, but volunteered no reason for his sudden decision to go into Listow, and Valerie could not bring herself to ask. The disloyalty of her feelings troubled her; Robin did not have to tell her where he was going, but he had always done so before.

As the taxi was heard coming up the drive, he looked at Valerie intently. He moved towards her as the noise of the engine grew louder.

Valerie forced a smile.

'I'm going into Listow to see the police,' said Robin, at last. 'I want to talk about one or two things with them, and I don't want it to be a family conference. Can you put up with William for a few hours?'

'Of course,' said Valerie. 'Darling, what – oh, it doesn't matter!' She turned away, and added: 'You'd better hurry, if you're going to catch that train.'

'I'll catch it,' Robin said. He put his arms about her. 'Look happy, my sweet! It will all work out satisfactorily, I assure you of that! One of the things I mean to tackle Webb about is this damn silly suspicion of you. It's unbearable! Confound it, I won't have them worrying you!'

'Robin,' said Valerie, steadily. 'You can't stop the police suspecting any of us. All I ask you is – tell them the truth. There's something you haven't told them, or me for that matter. Perhaps you think it's better that I don't know. Well, that's up to you. But don't try to deceive them, Robin. You won't succeed, and you'll only make things worse for yourself.'

Robin stared at her intently for a minute, and then kissed her, so fiercely that it made her breathless. Abruptly, he turned away and hurried through the passage towards the hall.

Valerie stood still, with tears in her eyes. She did not want to be seen by any of the others, but she did want to catch a glimpse of Robin as he went out.

From the passage door, she saw Robin stepping on to the porch. Then Charles joined him.

'Going places, Bob?' He sounded casual.

Robin, started.

'Oh, just as far as the station, to catch the 2.30 for Listow,' he said, with an obvious attempt to sound as casual as Charles. 'I want to get one or two things.'

Charles said: 'So do I. Have you room for me?'

There was only a split second's hesitation before Robin's, 'Of course!'

The taxi drove off with them both, and Valerie returned thoughtfully to the kitchen. She had not been there for more than two minutes before William came awkwardly into the room. He had been in the kitchen only once before, and then, as now, he gave the impression that he was out of his element. He glanced swiftly in her direction and Valerie knew instinctively that he disliked, perhaps 'resented' her.

'Did I see Robin and Charles leaving the house?' he asked in the almost playful voice of false geniality.

'Probably,' said Valerie, indifferently. 'They've gone into Listow.'

William stared; his eyes protuberant, his full lips pushed forward.

'Well!' he exclaimed. 'That really is too bad! They knew that *I* wanted to go!'

On the verge of saying more, he suppressed it. Turning, he stalked off, a picture of offended dignity. Why, thought Valerie wonderingly, had three of them suddenly decided to go into Listow? She was still wondering when she went upstairs, passing Lynda's room she glimpsed her lying on her bed with a book propped up on her pillow.

'Is that you, Val?' called Lynda. 'Why the sudden exodus, do you know?'

'Robin said that he wanted to see the police,' said Valerie.

Lynda stared at her.

'Poor Val! But I can't believe that Robin hasn't a good answer to everything.' She smiled, and there was genuine friendliness in her eyes. 'I have known him rather longer than you, Val. Don't worry too much.'

Valerie, tears in her eyes, left the room without speaking. Sympathy – the *necessity* for sympathy – was intolerable. Lynda stared thoughtfully at the door, then shrugged her shoulders and returned to her book. But she did not read with much concentration, being alert for every sound. They were few enough, although twice she heard William walking about downstairs, like a caged lion. Poor William!

Valerie sat in front of her dressing table mirror wiping her eyes. She was finding it too easy to cry. Her nerves were on edge and she had not had a minute's real peace since the police had arrived.

What had come over Robin?

In spite of herself, she let her mind wander to the early days of their courtship – those breathless, laughing, glorious days. The Robin who had come back to her was only the shell of the man she had then known.

Had he changed; or had he really been indifferent to her all the time, only wanting her for a specific purpose connected with those beastly crimes? Everything within her cried out against the very idea, but it would not be dismissed. Each member of the family became a sinister figure in a plot in which she was deeply involved and from which she might never extricate herself.

The atmosphere of the house was oppressive; the still watchfulness stifled her. She felt an overwhelming urge to get away, for however short a time. She then put on a light coat and went downstairs, going out the back way to avoid being seen. William was pacing the hall; he seemed distraught. She hated the sight of the man.

She slipped through the garden and over the stile leading to the church.

There, at least, she was likely to find sanctuary and mental rest. Yet, as she drew nearer, she saw a man briefly outlined in the porch.

She had not seen him before.

He was flashily dressed, his hair oiled, his features unprepossessing. She could imagine no one less likely to frequent a church.

He stared at her inimically for a moment or two, and then turned on his heel, taking the path which led away from the village.

The church was dark and cool and very quiet. Resting quietly in its soothing gloom, she heard a side door opening.

Frend came in.

His face, caught momentarily in the full light of a window, looked gaunt and strained. He did not see her, and going straight to the altar knelt in prayer.

After what seemed a long while, he stood up.

Again, the light fell full on his face. All sign of strain and trouble had gone. Strength and peace were there. Valerie felt humbled, exalted, as if for a moment, she too, had been touched by some Presence.

Then Frend saw her.

He smiled and approached, showing no sign of being startled, or sorry that she had been a witness of so intimate an experience.

'Hallo, Mrs Fayne!' he said. 'I didn't know you were here.' His voice was pitched low. 'I am grieved too, about what is happening, but I'm sure that it will work out happily for you.'

They were not polite words of reassurance; he meant what he said, and the words soothed her.

'You're very good,' she said.

'I doubt whether I am being as helpful as I should be,' he said, 'I would have suggested that you came here to pray, but I thought it was a battle that you had best work out for yourself.'

'It – it has helped,' she said; and it was a fact that she felt calmer, but it was more the effect of the transformation she had witnessed, than anything from within.

Frend smiled with gentle impersonality.

'I'll walk with you part of the way, if I may,' he said.

She reached the house at the same time that Robin, in Listow, was peering at Webb from the corner of the alley.

Chapter 19

One Canvas Recovered

Webb forgot that Folly was waiting at the shop door, as he stepped into the room where Crow lay. The face was turned away from Webb, and there was blood on the back of the neck.

Webb went down on one knee.

Crow was clutching a rolled-up canvas in his right hand, and his knuckles were white.

Without any possible chance or doubt, Webb saw that he was dead.

Slowly, he straightened up, and as he did so became aware too late, that if the picture dealer was dead, there was someone near, terribly near, who was very much alive. The blow, struck without a word, flung him forward over Crow's body.

Dazed, he lay there, dimly aware of noises, of muttering, and finally of steps approaching – familiar steps in their dainty pattering, at which he had often secretly laughed.

A hand lifted him.

'Here!' exclaimed Folly.

Webb staggered to his feet.

'Back door!' he muttered. 'Went out – back door!'

'Right!' said Folly.

From what seemed to be miles and miles away, Webb heard directions given, and then Folly was back.

A shrewd and penetrating voice said: 'You look a lot worse than you are. You scared me for a minute.'

'Scared?' asked Webb, bemusedly.

'Never mind, for now,' said Folly, with brisk sympathy. 'Do you feel all right?'

'Not exactly what I would call all right – but did you get him?'

'The answer is no,' said Folly angrily. 'If you had not looked so convincingly dead I might have had a chance.

Still, it can't be helped.' He looked down dispassionately at Crow. 'Violent death of a picture dealer,' he added. 'This isn't a nice case, Webb. Deeper than we thought. What's he got in his hand?'

He bent down and pulled at the roll of canvas in Crow's hand, very gently, prised open the dead man's fingers.

'A canvas,' declared Folly. He began to unroll it, 'Hum! Not up to much.'

It was the portrait of a man whom neither of them recognised. Folly who obviously knew more about pictures than he professed, examined it closely, rubbing his thumb gently over the surface.

'Varnish taken off recently,' he said. 'Ah – ' he looked down at the floor and, saw a rumpled rag and a corked bottle of methylated spirits. 'Reconstruction, Webb! Crow was cleaning the varnish off this thing. Working fast, crude stuff to use. Furtive fellow, but intent on his task. In creeps the killer. Poof!'

Webb attempted a fairly successful smile.

'Nothing unusual in a dealer cleaning off a picture, is there?'

'Most unusual. It takes an expert – though Crow might have fancied himself as one. The time he chose to start work is the thing.' Folly sniffed heartily. 'When we first saw Crow, was there any particular smell?'

'The place was pretty fusty,' said Webb. 'I don't remember anything else.'

'You didn't smell anything else, because it wasn't there to smell. You would have noticed if methylated spirits had been used. Therefore, as soon as we went, he must have started to use it. Nothing sinful in that, but it's curious. He might have been getting the varnish soft to make the canvas flexible enough for rolling – rolling doesn't hurt the paint if there's no hard surface of varnish to crack it. Usual system is to brush the thing over with methylated, which softens everything but the paint.'

Webb eyed him in unfeigned admiration.

'You're good!' he said. 'And there's another – '

Gently, happily, Folly's ego inflated, his eyes half shut. 'If Crow suddenly got scared and started to get a canvas or so ready for rolling, it suggests that he wanted to hide them,' he murmured. 'So, they might have been those from The Paddocks. If this is one of them, where are the others? You didn't see who attacked you, I suppose?'

Webb grimaced. 'I did not, *but* – ' he eyed Folly thoughtfully – 'I saw a man at the end of the alley, who almost certainly had just left the shop. One of our suspects,' he added, cunningly prolonging the suspense.

'Hell and high-water, *who*?' howled Folly.

'Robin Fayne,' said Webb, and sat back to enjoy himself.

Folly did not disappoint him. He rose to his full and majestic height and crashed a clenched fist on the desk.

'Beautiful! Glorious! Fayne absolutely wide open for anything we can give him – Webb dear boy, I hand it to you! No chance of a mistake I suppose?' he added, anxiously. 'No guesswork? You wouldn't be trying to put one over a simple representative of the Yard?'

'Don't be an ass!' said Webb, daring in his happiness. 'Mind you, I didn't see him leave the shop or the garden, but he was certainly in the alley. I *think* he saw me.'

'Could he have come back and slogged you?'

Webb shook his head, 'Unlikely, I should say.'

'But what a scoop!' cried Folly in uninhibited delight. 'Mysterious visitors to the shop, one of them identified. Don't tell me that I'm flogging the obvious – I know I am. Have to, sometimes. So Fayne and the second man could have killed Crow. Good.'

Webb glanced at the dead man.

'Good?' His voice was sardonic.

'Come! It isn't Crow, any more. Just a corpse,' cried Folly, armed now against pity, his defences well nigh impregnable. 'Some measure of blame is ours, but face it frankly. We know that it was only an idea that brought us here. An idea that came too late. Result – we've found Crow at least two or three hours earlier than was likely. He might even have lain here all night. He was a bachelor, wasn't he?'

'Yes,' said Webb, 'he lived on his own.'

'Oh, we can bless our lucky stars! No mysterious murder of Mottram to occupy our minds to the exclusion of all else!' Folly's mind at this moment was a bloodhound's mind. No extraneous thought or emotion must touch the one predominating instinct. 'Find Crow's murderer, and it will lead to Mottram's. Yes, it's *much* better. And Fayne – ' Folly looked dreamily towards the ceiling, which was streaked with cracks in the plaster – 'had the opportunity for both murders. We'd better work on Fayne. Mind if I go out to The Paddocks while you look after things here?'

'Of course not.'

'Good man! When you feel up to it, come out to The Paddocks. I won't make any arrests on my own. Promise! Oh, and that man Unwin. No Crow for him to watch so it might be as well for him to lie low until we want a man the locals won't recognise. Can I leave that to you too?'

'Yes,' said Webb, and added with a sudden grin: 'You can also borrow my car.' He took a key from a ring and handed it to Folly.

Back in his office, busying himself with the formalities of the new investigation, Webb found himself wondering about Valerie Fayne. His inclination was to believe that she was both a victim of circumstances and of conspiracy, but he was sensible enough to know that he was largely influenced by her appearance. Yet Lynda Mottram was the more beautiful woman and he had no such sympathy towards her – only a healthy respect for her quick-wittedness.

If Valerie Fayne were putting on an act she had little chance of deceiving Folly.

The woman was either all that she professed to be or even cleverer than Lynda Mottram.

His thoughts travelled on to Robin Fayne, whose presence at Crow's shop was going to take so much explaining; as was his whole attitude. He –

Webb's eyes widened.

'Why was he in such a hurry to get married?' he asked aloud.

The more Webb thought of it, the more he considered it possible that the marriage had not taken place only because they had fallen in love with each other.

Fayne had risked offending his uncle, who held the money bags. His explanation to Folly had been plausible, but full of holes. In spite of all the adverse circumstances, he had rushed Valerie into marriage and, within a few days of their settling in at The Padocks, this business had started.

Had Fayne known it was going to start? Had he actually planned it? Was it possible that he had married Valerie because he knew a wife was not bound to give evidence against her husband?

The idea obsessed Webb. He was still thinking it over when the telephone rang.

'P.C. Carrow of Pelham, is asking for you, sir,' said the operator. 'Will you speak to him?'

'Put him through,' said Webb, and added after a brief pause: 'Yes, Carrow, what can I do for you?'

The Pelham policeman's voice was hoarse with excitement.

'I thought you ought to know about this at *once*, sir.'

'That's all right,' said Webb. 'What's happened?'

'Chesterton's back, *sir*!' breathed Carrow. 'You know, Mr Dering's gardener. And there's another thing.'

'Go on,' said Webb, scribbling excitedly on a pad as he listened. '*What's* that?'

'Absolutely certain I am, sir,' said Carrow, 'she left The Paddocks –'

'You mean Mrs Fayne?'

'Mrs *Fayne* went from The Paddocks,' said Carrow, with elaborate emphasis, 'and walked to the church. Soon after she'd gone into the churchyard, Chesterton was seen to come *out*, by another gate, sir. If you ask me –'

'Did anyone telephone The Paddocks?' cut in Webb, sharply.

'Not to my knowledge, sir.'

'Make sure, will you? Is there anything else?'

'That's the lot, sir,' said Carrow, 'except that the vicar was seen to go in soon afterwards.'

'You've done very well, Carrow,' said Webb. 'I'll see you later.'

He rang off.

So. If Valerie Fayne had gone to the church to keep an appointment with Chesterton, it would be the beginning of the end of her protestations of complete innocence. Frend's visit was normal enough, but it was curious that it had taken place at such a moment.

All these things faded into insignificance against another possibility, and again he wished that Folly were at hand to express his opinion. For it occurred to Webb that Robin Fayne might, in fact, be trying to protect his wife rather than his wife be scheming to protect him.

Chapter 20

Robin Returns to The Paddocks

Valerie returned to the house, still uplifted by her experience in the church.

Her suspicion of Robin had lost much of its sting.

She was sure now, that some quixotic motive was at the back of the whole thing, and that he would explain everything to her just as soon as possible. She was humming to herself as she went past Lynda's door.

'Feeling better?' Lynda called.

'Oh, very much so,' said Valerie, going in. 'I've been for a walk and blown some of the fears away, but I hope it won't be long before we can return to normal.'

'You're telling me!' Lynda swung her shapely legs from the bed, and stretched herself. 'What a mess I look!' she exclaimed, grimacing at herself in the mirror.

'I wish I looked half as lovely,' Valerie said, generously. 'You're coming down to tea?'

'Yes, of course. Every time William opens his mouth, I want to throw something in it. Buns will be almost irrestible.'

Valerie laughed, but as she went downstairs she was a little disturbed. Lynda was certainly amusing, but there was undoubtedly animosity at the root. As it happened, William had a headache and asked if he could have a cup of tea in his room.

Valerie was brewing another pot of tea when she heard a voice call out cautiously:

'Battley, can you spare a minute?'

'I be here, if I be wanted,' answered Battley, stoutly.

Glancing out of the kitchen window, Valerie saw that Carrow and a Listow policeman were approaching. The sight of Carrow was always enough to make Battley obstructive. She smiled to herself as the three men met.

The Listow policeman said something in an undertone,

obviously not wanting to be heard by anyone in the kitchen, but Battley promptly undid his effort, by declaring in a loud voice:

'No, I haven't heard the telephone.'

'Are you *sure?*'

'Course I be sure.'

Valerie picked up the tray and went out, but the incident had clouded the outlook again, and reminded her that they were under constant surveillance.

About six o'clock, a car turned into the drive. Valerie's heart leapt at the thought that Robin had returned. But it was Webb's Morris, and in it the detective from Scotland Yard.

She led him into the drawing room, without speaking.

Folly said pleasantly:

'There are several questions which I want to ask your husband, Mrs Fayne. Is he in?'

'No,' said Valerie, more poignantly than she realised. Robin had said that he was going to see the police and she had taken him at his word; now, she knew that he had not gone to Listow for that purpose, and her mind was in a turmoil again.

Folly looked at her shrewdly.

'Do you know where he is?'

'He went into Listow this afternoon,' she said.

'Alone?'

'His brother was with him – and before you ask me, I will tell you that I have no idea when they will be back,' Valerie said sharply.

'I believe a train is due in shortly,' said Folly. 'I'll wait a little, if I may. And there are one or two things I'd like to look at in the attic, Mrs Fayne.'

She went with him as far as the first floor, watching him climb, with his curiously light tread, the narrow staircase to the attic. As soon as he disappeared, William and Lynda emerged from their rooms. William held a finger to his lips, enjoining silence, and they went downstairs together.

In the hall, William said:

'What does he want this time?'

'He says he wants to see Robin.'

'Then he has probably come for some other purpose, the man is incapable of telling the truth,' declared William righteously. He looked at Lynda, with a worried and distracted frown. 'Lynda, I hope you and I will bury the hatchet during such times as these. When he joins us, I will be glad if you will leave the talking to me.'

'Do you really think he'd let us, even if we wanted to?' marvelled Lynda, half smiling at the childishness of pompous men.

'At least have the sense not to tell him I have sent for Feldmann, my solicitor,' William said tartly, his attitude slipping back into his normal one of impatient condescension. Valerie did not answer.

She hoped that Robin would get back before Folly returned, but there was still no sign of him when Folly came down.

William rose to his full height, but Folly was taller, and the more imposing.

'I trust, Superintendent,' said William in a forbidding voice, 'that you have some news for us?'

Folly smiled. 'Not yet, I'm afraid. Had you anything particular in mind?'

'You know very well that it is preposterous to suspect anyone here of the murder of my uncle,' said William. 'I am hoping to have your assurance that you are concentrating elsewhere in your investigations.'

Folly allowed these grandiloquent words to disperse unheeded into the room, as he slowly unfurled a bulky parcel, and drew out a roll of canvas. 'There's just one thing I would like to know,' he said. 'Is this familiar?'

He watched all three.

William frowned; Lynda remained expressionless; Valerie's eyes widened as she saw the portrait which Folly unrolled, she took a step forward.

'That's one of the canvases!' she exclaimed.

'What canvases?' asked Folly, blandly.

'Those that were stolen, of course,' said Valerie. 'I recognise the face – where did you get it?'

'Ah-ha!' Folly was childish. 'That would be telling! But I'm very glad to hear you say so, Mrs Fayne. I *thought* it was one of the missing paintings, but I couldn't be sure.' He rolled it up again, and seemed to lose all interest in the matter. 'Has Mr Frend been here this afternoon?'

'No,' said Valerie.

'I wonder – ' Folly paused. 'No, I won't go and see him.

I'll wait for Mr Fayne. But please don't let me interfere with what you are doing.'

Valerie assured him, mechanically, that he was not interfering with their plans. But she distrusted Folly in this childish, friendly mood. He seemed more dangerous – as if he had something to spring on them, and was deliberately making the preparations for it.

At last, Parker's taxi turned into the drive.

Folly's great bulk rose from his chair as if without bones or joints, and approached the window. Valerie saw that it was Robin, sitting next to Parker; Charles was not with him.

The taxi drew up and Robin stepped out.

Folly, gliding from the sitting-room with uncanny precision, was in the porch to greet him.

Valerie could just see Robin's startled face. It was very apparent that Folly was the last man he had wanted to see. They eyed each other in silence for an appreciable time. Then Robin turned and paid off Parker.

'Good-evening.' He sounded cold and aloof.

'Good-evening,' repeated Folly, as coldly, as aloof. 'I'm very glad that you're back, Mr Fayne. I have been waiting for you for some time.'

'What is it?' Robin asked, carefully.

'One or two matters which I hope you will be able to explain to everyone's satisfaction,' said Folly. 'Where is the most convenient place?'

Watching Robin's set face, Valerie knew that he was afraid. His youth, his vulnerability, went to her heart. Not only was he incapable of outwitting Folly, but he was inviting trouble all the time he tried. And she wanted to help him; his evasions and deceits counted for nothing, and what he had done was unimportant.

They walked towards the morning-room, and Valerie on impulse, followed.

'Robin!' she called.

He turned and looked at her; and just for a moment Valerie saw on his face an expression of sheer horror – not fear, but horror. It passed in a flash, but she knew that he was labouring under the strain of a great emotion.

'I'll be back soon,' he said. 'I'm having a word with the great panjandrum!' The attempt at jocularity was woefully weak, and he seemed to realise it. He looked away from her as he walked out, Folly stalking like an inescapable fate, beside him.

The morning-room door close after them.

Valerie turned and went upstairs.

The two men stood stiffly face to face.

'Well?' Robin said, harshly.

'*Well*, Mr Fayne,' said Folly, gently. 'And where have you been?'

'Into Listow. What business is it of yours?'

'It has a great deal to do with me,' said Folly. 'Where did you go?'

'I refuse to answer your questions!'

'Are you well-advised to adopt this attitude?' asked Folly, very softly. 'Hadn't you better tell me where you've been and what you've been doing? Come, now! Think hard! I am a police officer, Mr Fayne. My duty is the hounding down of criminals. In the course of that duty, I often uncover most unpleasant private and personal matters – skeletons in the cupboards, shall I say? It is all part of my duty, but I do not disclose such discoveries unless they are connected with the case in hand. I am seeking a murderer. Your behaviour, allied to other matters, makes me suspect that you know more about it than you profess.'

'I suppose you have some reason for this peroration?' Robin said, coldly. 'If so, I'd like to know what it is.'

'So you won't be wise?' said Folly, shaking his head regretfully. 'Such a pity. Have you, by any chance, been looking for – this?'

He stretched forward the furled canvas unrolling it quickly while he looked into Robin's eyes. Robin started. Then he drew back, as if knowing that he had betrayed himself.

Folly snapped: 'Where are the others?'

Robin stared at him, his eyes dull.

'Where are they?' pressed Folly. 'You went to get them from Crow's shop! You were seen coming away. What did you kill him with, Fayne? What weapon did you use?'

Robin cleared his throat.

'I – I didn't kill him. I went to get the canvases, yes. They didn't belong to him. They were – the family's.'

'I see. You were so anxious to get half-a-dozen third-rate oil paintings that you went to Crow's shop, demanded them with menace, and, when he refused to give them to you, killed him.'

'I didn't kill him,' said Robin, flatly.

'No-o?' Folly's tone was silky with disbelief. 'I suppose you got there and found him dead?'

'That – is so.' Robin hesitated only for a moment.

'Very convenient for you,' said Folly. 'You found him dead and the pictures there for the taking.'

'I didn't find the pictures,' Robin said. 'I got there and found Crow dead. He had one canvas in his hand. I didn't try to find out whether it was one of ours.'

'*Very* restraining of you,' conceded Folly. 'Why were you so anxious to get the pictures? Their value is – ' he raised a hand – 'negligible! Hardly worth the paint used on them.'

Robin stepped to the side of the room, and leaned against an easy chair. He ran his hand through his hair, obviously trying to collect himself. He did not answer immediately, and when he did his voice lacked conviction.

'They have great sentimental value.'

'To you?'

'To the family.'

'You were willing to take this great risk in order to recover sentimental trash for a family you – in part at least – heartily dislike, when the police could have regained them for you with no trouble at all? Is that what you are asking me to believe?'

Robin said: 'You can believe what you like. I went to see Crow to get the pictures. I knew he had them. He – '

'How did you know?'

'That's my business.'

'You'll soon learn that it's mine, too,' said Folly. 'You'll soon learn that you have made a great many mistakes, Mr Fayne. But let us, for the moment, assume that Crow was dead when you got there. How did you get in?'

'The front door was open.'

'The *shop* door, Mr Fayne?'

'Yes.'

'Remarkable!' exclaimed Folly. 'It was locked very soon afterwards. Or did you lock the door when you discovered Mr Crow was dead?'

'I didn't lock the door,' said Robin. 'I didn't know it was locked.'

'Then why did you go out the back way?'

'Because – ' Robin paused. 'Because I preferred not to be seen. But – ' he paused again, searching for words. 'I glanced round and saw Webb. I didn't know whether he'd seen me, but I knew that if it were known that I had been near Crow's house at the time he was killed, some parallel would be drawn between his death and my uncle's. I hoped to avoid – incurring further – suspicions.' The words came out stiffly.

'So you do know you have done so?' said Folly. 'You didn't think how much better it would have been for you had you come to report?'

Robin said nothing.

'A truly remarkable thing,' said Folly. 'If I had gone into that shop and seen a murdered man, realising that sooner or later the police would discover I had been there, *I* would not have run off, I certainly would not.'

Robin kept silent.

'Unless, of course, I'd had a very strong reason for it,' went on Folly softly. 'Now, in your position, what would have been a strong enough reason to make me run off I wonder!' He looked narrowly at Robin.

'I've given you my reason,' Robin's voice rose to a slightly higher note.

'I'm not satisfied with it, Mr Fayne! I shall require you to come to Listow with me and make a statement. Amongst the other things I shall want to know is – *who* else was in the shop, besides you and Crow?'

'I saw no one,' muttered Robin.

It was quite obvious that he was lying. It was clear, too, that he was not surprised by Folly's decision, and he appeared resigned to going into Listow. Their immediate departure, however, was delayed by the arrival of Sir Percy Feldmann.

Folly, recognising the familiar pale face of the solicitor, knew that this arrival might lead to difficulties that he would not be able to overcome without detaining Robin formally.

'And I don't think it's quite time for that,' mused Folly to himself. 'Still, we'll see.'

Chapter 21

Feldmann Disappoints

Valerie had anticipated the arrival of Sir Percy Feldmann with deep longing. Robin had failed her; Charles had made no serious attempt to challenge authority; William, obsessed with his own sense of importance had disappointed her beyond words. She had thought that a solicitor would know precisely how to handle, and subdue, the police.

At first sight the solicitor proved to be a disappointing man, bony, lustreless and pale. Valerie hoped fervently but with lessening conviction that, like an iceberg, his strength was yet to be revealed.

Folly contrived to be at hand when Feldmann entered the lounge, and Valerie went out soon afterwards, called by Robin in a low-pitched, strangled voice which sent a surge of alarm through her. He had aged in the past few hours; whatever had happened in Listow had engraved deep lines on his face.

In search of privacy they set off for a short walk through the grounds. With a catch at her heart Valerie noticed that one of Webb's men was keeping within easy reach of them. Robin was aware of it too, and kept sending quick, anxious glances towards the man. He did not speak for some minutes, apparently trying to make up his mind what to say. Then, abruptly:

'Val, everything's gone wrong. The police are going to take me into Listow for further questioning.'

'Robin!' She stared at him, gripping his arm tightly. 'Robin – ' her voice faltered.

'Everything's gone wrong,' Robin repeated. 'Val, there's something I can't tell you, yet. I will as soon as this is over.' He added quickly: 'A man was murdered in Listow this afternoon. I found him.'

Valerie stared at him, her heart beating so quickly that she felt she could hardly breathe.

'He was an acquaintance of my uncle's.' Robin had difficulty in getting the words out. 'I don't know why he was killed, but the police connect the two crimes. Like a damned fool, I ran away, instead of reporting to the police. Webb saw me.'

Valerie said nothing, but tightened her grip on his arm. He covered her hand with his and for the first time summoned a smile.

'So you see, I had the opportunity to commit both murders. It's not surprising that they're after me.'

Valerie said: 'Darling, did you *know* that Uncle Silas had been murdered?'

There was a long pause. The policeman, twenty yards away from them, gazed intently at a small flock of sparrows. The silence grew prolonged, unbearable. Valerie drew a deep breath and spoke quietly:

'Did you know?'

He said: 'I'm not going to answer that, Val. I've finished telling you lies, or half lies. I'm not going to answer questions unless I can tell you the whole truth, and I can't do that yet. I did not kill either of them.' He turned and looked at her, his eyes unexpectedly calm, sober and questioning. 'You believe that, don't you?'

'Of course I do!'

'Bless you!' said Robin, smiling more freely. 'It's been the very devil of a thing to be pitch-forked into, but I'll get you out of it as quickly as I can. Meanwhile, they might keep me in Listow for a day or two. Heaven knows, they've reason enough! You can rely on Feldmann – he'll look after the legal end of it. William's gone to pieces, but that's not unusual. Charles –' he paused. 'Give Charles all the help you can. He may need it. Will you do that?'

Valerie said: 'Is it going to harm you if I do?'

'Please do what I ask! I must feel that he has someone on whom he can rely, whatever happens. Will you promise me?'

She hesitated, then said at last:

'Yes, Robin.' Her voice sounded flat and unnecessarily subdued.

'Bless you!' he said again. 'Now Charles is –'

He stopped, for there was a shout from the farther side of the drive. A second cry followed, then a third.

Someone appeared on the porch, and a policeman raced

past them. Robin quickened his pace, gripping Valerie's arm.

A man appeared out of the shrubs, running unevenly, with his head thrown back and his fists clenched. Stocky and flashily dressed, Valerie knew at once that she had seen him before.

He reached the drive and hesitated, then turned towards the gates.

The bushes parted again, and Charles burst through, in hot pursuit. As the fugitive reached the gates, Webb's car appeared nosing its way slowly into the drive. The running man hesitated for a moment, then dived between the car and the nearside post. As he passed the driver he aimed a vicious punch, and the car, momentarily out of control hit the gate with a resounding crash.

Still in hot pursuit Charles vaulted over the bonnet of the obstructing car, and was lost to sight.

'Robin!' cried Valerie. 'Don't follow him, don't!'

She did not know whether the warning, or the difficulty of getting over the obstruction stopped him; certainly something did. Webb and the driver extricated themselves with a certain amount of difficulty, and together with the help of Folly – hastily brought to the scene by the sound of the crash – they managed to steer the wreckage to the side of the road.

Folly, mopping his perspiring brow, turned to Valerie:

'Who – was – it?'

'One – one was Charles,' said Valerie.

'Charles? Oh – Commander Fayne! Oh. Who was – the other?'

'I don't know,' said Valerie. 'I saw him this afternoon, but –'

'*I* know who he is,' said a voice from behind them.

They turned, equally startled, to see Battley. He looked dour and old, struck down by some knowledge or experience, even as Robin had been.

Folly said, almost gently:

'Who is it?'

'Chesterton,' said Battley.

To Valerie, the name was unfamiliar, but it conveyed something to Folly. An enigmatic mask slid over any satisfaction or surprise he might feel.

'Ha!' he exclaimed, 'the improbable Chesterton. When did you last see him, Battley?'

'A while back,' said Battley, as willing to hide all emotion as Folly, but less successful. 'Three weeks, maybe, and naught else 'til he ran out of that hedge as if the de'il himself was on his tail. I hope he was!' added Battley, harshly.

'No love for Chesterton, eh?' said Folly. 'Who was chasing who?'

'No Mottram ever ran from the likes of 'un,' said Battley, with great dignity, 'nor ever will.'

'So your brother-in-law was chasing Chesterton,' said Folly, smiling at Valerie. 'Quite an interesting little development, don't you think? *Quite* interesting!' His beam was as impersonal as if he had bought half a dozen, and was methodically using them up. He looked round as Lynda, William and Feldmann approached.

'I wonder where they've gone?' Lynda voiced the question which was in all of their minds.

'We'll know in good time,' said Folly, as if he were on familiar terms with providence. 'Don't you worry about that, Miss Mottram.'

Valerie's only relief was that Robin was still free. She feared that if he were once taken into custody, he would not be released. She could see that there was a strong case against him, and, to her, his expression alone had given the lie to his protests of innocence. Why had he been such a fool?

Yet – there was some slight comfort in the fact that he had lost no time in joining Webb in the pursuit of Chesterton.

How strange that she had met the man at the church – and that he had given the impression that he had wanted to speak to her.

She had disliked and distrusted him at sight. Surely there was evil there, and the police would recognise it? Hoping that they might see in him a greater and more demonstrable suspect than they saw in Robin, she went back to the house to wait.

Chapter 22

Chesterton's Misfortune

Webb had caught up with Robin, who was following a clearly-defined track in the long grass of a meadow nearly ready for cutting.

'This way,' he grunted.

He led the way through a group of trees to a field where the young green shoots of wheat were already ankle high. Someone had run across there, as carelessly as across the meadow, Robin paused on the edge and gazed across.

Pelham lay stretched out in front of them, the spire of the church high and clear against the sky, and next to it, the roof of the vicarage.

Webb could see a man not far from the church. To get to him, it would be better to walk along the side of the field. As they hurried on, Webb saw that it was Charles Fayne.

Beside the white and grey gravestones, Charles stood motionless.

Apparently he knew that the others were approaching, for when they were still fifty yards from him, he turned and waved the stick which he had been carrying.

'Lost him!' he said, succinctly.

'Who was it?' demanded Webb.

'Gardener-wallah, who used to work at The Paddocks,' said Charles, casually.

Webb looked meaningly at the stick.

'Oh, that,' said Charles. 'I'd picked it up as I was crossing one of the paddocks, and it was just as well. He'd have bowled me over if I hadn't lashed out with it.' Charles smiled, broadly. 'Whose car did I climb over?' he added, amiably. 'There'll be a few scratches on the paint, I'm afraid.'

'It was a police car,' said Webb. 'Have you any idea where he went?'

'I could have sworn that he reached the churchyard,' said Charles. 'Is it worth searching, do you think?'

'Come on!'

There were three paths in the churchyard. They took one apiece, but all reached the far end without seeing a trace of their quarry.

The door of the church was standing open; peace and tranquillity and timelessness lay everywhere, compelling men to lay down the burden of their feverish hates and anxieties.

'Nothing here,' said Charles, in a small, quiet voice. 'I don't know that I like looking for a suspect in a church anyway.'

'Do you know where the vestry is?' asked Webb.

'On the right,' said Robin.

'Stay here, if you prefer to.'

Webb went forward, walking firmly along the aisle, slowly followed by Robin and Charles.

'Any luck?' asked Charles, in a low-pitched voice, as he neared the vestry.

'No, nothing here,' said Webb. 'I wish –'

He stopped abruptly as the outer door opened and the tall gaunt figure of Frend appeared.

'Please forgive our intrusion,' murmured Robin courteously, after a swift look at Webb, who, either unaware of being in the wrong, or unwilling to admit it, was staring silently at Frend.

Charles said pleasantly:

'We've had a spot of bother at The Paddocks again, and thought the culprit took refuge in here.'

'Here?' Frend looked icily at a row of flattened surplices which could have hidden nothing stouter than an attenuated bat. 'Surely not? You've seen no one?'

'No,' said Webb, stiffly. 'Have you, Mr Frend?'

'Certainly,' answered Frend calmly. 'But before I give you an exhausting list of parishioners it might be less fatiguing to tell me for whom you are looking.'

'Chesterton – Dering's gardener,' said Charles, promptly.

'Chesterton?' Frend's expression was one of polite inquiry. 'I understand that he had returned to London.'

Webb, either deceived, or pretending to be deceived, by the evasiveness of this remark, they left the vicar and walked on to the lych gate. Here they stood for a few seconds, looking over the vicarage orchard, but there was no sign of movement.

Approaching unheard over the soft ground P.C. Carrow tapped Webb smartly on the arm. Impassively, yet with a rich sense of importance, he reported:

'Have seen Chesterton, sir.'

'*Chesterton?* Where, man, where?'

'Battley's cottage, sir.'

'Are you *sure?*'

'Quite sure, sir. Keeping my eyes open, as directed, I observed him sneaking in the back way.'

Webb turned at a lumbering run. 'Come on!'

Reaching the garden gate, he waved a hand towards the side of the cottage.

'One of you wait there,' he said to the two following policemen, 'the other go to the back door.'

'Are we in the way?' asked Charles.

Webb shook his head impatiently.

He did not knock, but raised the latch of the door, and it opened without trouble. He stood on the threshold for a minute, listening, then moving rapidly, he searched the downstair rooms. Both were empty.

'It looks as though he's gone,' said Webb, tensely. 'I'll have a look upstairs.'

Taking the stairs at a bound he looked into one of the rooms, and had half-turned to the other when Charles yelled:

'Look out. Webb!'

Instantly Webb jumped sideways. The down-sweeping blow, missing his head by inches glanced off his shoulder. Chesterton, staggering forward, a poker in his hand stood glaring at him.

Before he could strike again Charles was on him. The poker clattered harmlessly to the ground. Chesterton clapped his hands to his stomach, gasping for breath.

Charles stood back.

'So we've got the merchant! He wields a pretty poker, doesn't he?'

'Thanks,' Webb said, briefly. 'I want you, Chesterton.'

The man groaned, while under cover of half-shut lids his eyes shiftily assessed his chances of escape.

As Webb moved a step nearer, Chesterton kicked out at him. Charles shot his right foot out and Chesterton, tripping over it, sprawled forward, banging his head. This time there was no shamming, and he lay semi-conscious and incapable of further resistance, on the floor.

Webb threw Charles a quick, appreciative glance.

'Thanks again,' he said, with a faint smile.

The room was in chaos, bedclothes strewn about the floor, pillows were slit, clothes which had been hanging behind the door torn from their hooks. Nothing seemed to have been left in its proper place. Ornaments had been swept from the mantelpiece. Even the faded blue curtains were off the rod, hanging askew.

'Well, well!' exclaimed Charles. 'Chesterton obviously wanted something. I wonder what he thought Battley kept hidden up here?'

'I wonder if he found anything?' said Robin. 'Isn't it time we looked through his pockets, Inspector?'

'I'll do it,' said Webb.

Idly watching him, Robin picked up a handful of feathers and let them fall, two or three at a time. When they had all gone he took another handful – and, as he did so, he felt something hard inside the pillow. It was small and had hard edges.

He gave it his full attention. Feathers began to float about the room, fluttering slowly downwards as he plunged his hands in their suffocating softness to grasp whatever was hidden there.

He believed he knew what it was as he drew out a square leather case.

'My oath!' exclaimed Charles. 'The necklace!'

Chapter 23

Battley's Denials

Chesterton struggled to his feet, but made no further attempt to get away. He seemed fascinated by the diamonds as Robin, dropping them on the bed, raised his hands helplessly.

'It's incredible!' he exclaimed. 'In *Battley's* pillow!'

Webb turned to Chesterton.

'Is that what you were looking for?' he asked sharply.

'Suppose it was?' growled Chesterton. 'And suppose it wasn't, see? I ain't saying nothing.'

Webb looked at him coldly, and repeated:

'Is that what you were looking for?'

'I ain't saying,' Chesterton said, truculently. 'I got m' rights. I thought you was a burglar, that's why I come at you, before that smarty started to get rough.' He glared resentfully at Charles.

'*Battley!*' exclaimed Robin, helplessly. 'I thought – '

'You got a lot to learn about that snake,' said Chesterton, viciously, ' 'e would 'ave bin in clink years ago if the police had known what they was doin' of. I thought you was a burglar,' he added, defiantly, 'I got every right to 'it a burglar, 'aven't I?'

Webb said: 'What right had you to be here at all?'

'I was looking for somefink wot Battley stole, that's wot I was looking for. Pickshers. A sneaking, lying, two-faced thief, that's Battley.'

'So you were looking for pictures, were you?' said Webb.

'Supposing I was?' demanded Chesterton, aggressively. 'They belonged to my guv'nor, I got the right to get my guv'nor's things back, ain't I?'

'Did you find them?' asked Webb.

'No, I never. But I reckon they're around, some place. Stole from my guv'nor, about a fortnight ago. I bin looking for them ever since.'

Webb wasted no more time talking to the man, but, after giving instructions to Carrow, returned with the gardener. Robin and Charles to The Paddocks. Battley, standing by the police car which had brought Webb from Listow, was quick to see them.

Webb called:

'Battley, come up to the house at once, will you?'

He and Chesterton were sent, in charge of Kennedy, to the morning-room, while Webb sought out Folly.

Folly waited until the door had closed on the curious and inquiring family, then said:

'Well, what's this little do about?'

Webb explained briefly. Folly nodded, rocking his great bulk from heel to toe.

'We are getting on. First the picture back and now the diamonds. Excellent, my dear Webb. Excellent! We know that Dering's in it somewhere, too, and Battley comes right into the front line.' He smiled delightedly. 'No love lost between Battley and Chesterton, do you say?'

'There certainly isn't!'

'Hum! Well, if you ask me, Webb, have a word with Charles Fayne, first. Don't tell me that he just happened to come across a man in the shrubbery and then set about him because he didn't like his face. Charles is no fool, you know. The Mottram girl's a cool 'un, but Charles – ye-es, *Charles* has got something. Shall we send for him?'

Webb grinned. 'Why ask me?'

'Protocol, dear boy, protocol. Always excellent in theory; and to be flourished on occasions.'

Summoned, Charles obeyed leisurely.

'At your service, gentlemen!' he said.

'Good!' exclaimed Folly. 'Having said it, I expect you to mean it, Commander Fayne. You will tell me, then, what Chesterton did to deserve that wallop you gave him across the face.'

'Wallop?' repeated Charles vaguely. 'Oh, *that*. He was lurking in the grounds, as I've said. Also – ' Charles raised one eyebrow – 'he had a trowel and was digging near a shrub. I startled him, but he's a powerful beggar and he nearly bowled me over. I grabbed at the branch of a tree and lammed him with it. Perfectly simple.'

'Digging, was he?' mused Folly. 'What for?'

'I haven't the faintest idea. There are so many exciting

things to dig for – bodies, pictures, diamonds – It must be difficult to choose.'

Folly said austerely:

'Just remember, please, that this isn't the time for being funny, you might be misunderstood. You've been in Listow this afternoon, haven't you?'

'I have,' said Charles.

'Did you see your brother there?'

'We went in together.'

'Did you *stay* together?'

'We did not. But aren't you questioning the wrong man? Chesterton must be getting impatient.'

'The wrong man? – What put that idea into your head?' asked Folly softly. 'Please answer my question. Where did you leave your brother?'

'At the station.'

'Where did he go?'

'I haven't the faintest idea.'

'Where did you go?' demanded Folly relentlessly.

'Oh, I went to see a picture dealer, named Crow,' said Charles, lightly. 'But the door was shut, and no one answered my knocking, so I came away again. Is there anything else you would like to know, Superintendent?'

Folly eyed him levelly, then turned away and told him there was nothing more for the moment. Charles bowed mockingly, and went back into the lounge.

Folly raised an eyebrow. 'I should say he was shaken just a little more than he appeared to be – but then again, that might be my overwhelming vanity. You must have noticed Webb, that no one is allowed to be plain vain, they must always be overwhelmingly so – now let's see what Battley and our friend Chesterton have to say.'

Battley was standing by the window of the morning-room, Chesterton, some feet away. He opened fire at once, with the aggression of a cornered man.

'Wot are yer keeping me 'ere for, that's wot I'd like to know. Innocent –'

Folly said authoritatively:

'Keep quiet! I'll tell you when I want you to speak.'

Webb knew that had he himself said the same thing in the same way, Chesterton would have retorted in kind. But now, Dering's gardener moved uneasily, his eyes darting to and fro, as he relapsed into silence.

Folly's voice grew milder.

'Now, Battley, I know you won't mind answering a few questions. This man was found in your cottage. Had he a key?'

Battley looked in cold, controlled hatred, at Chesterton.

'He had neither the key nor the right to be there,' he declared, steadily.

'I thought not. He claims that he was looking for some pictures that were stolen from his employer.'

'I know nothing of any pictures, sir.'

'He declares that he knows you stole them, some weeks ago.'

' 'Tis a lie,' said Battley.

Chesterton moved forward, clearing his throat. The Yard man shot him a glance which reduced him to a sullen silence.

'He had searched your bedroom thoroughly,' went on Folly, 'and damaged some of the bedding.'

'It's good fortune for him, sir, that it was you and not myself who caught him,' Battley said, thinly.

'You belly-aching old corpse!' Chesterton exploded. 'You wouldn't last ten seconds with me! You took them pickshers, and – '

'Silence!' roared Folly.

Chesterton gulped and dropped his clenched hands to his side. There was no doubt that he was frightened of the Yard man.

Folly said simply, even beguilingly, 'Tell me, Battley, did you keep anything that he might want, at the cottage?'

'Not that I knows of, sir.'

'Not even – ' Folly glanced meaningly at Webb, and tapped his inside pocket. 'Not even – ' he paused, as Webb put his hand in his pocket to take out the necklace. 'Not even *these*, Battley?'

The diamonds scintillated, and became the cynosure of all eyes, except Folly's – who was trying to look in every direction at once. He saw the incredulity in Battley's eyes – and he also saw the cunning glint which sprang to Chesterton's.

'The necklace – *that's the one he tried to sell me*!' The man's malicious face was aglow with triumph.

Folly snapped:

'Is that what you went to look for? The diamonds, not the pictures?'

Chesterton growled: 'Supposing it was? I ain't saying nothing, only that he offered them ter me. 'E thought my guv'nor might give a hundred quid for 'em!'

Folly said: 'Well Battley, what have you to say to that?'

Battley turned his narrowed eyes towards Chesterton. He appeared to contemplate the man mildly enough, but when he spoke there was hatred in his voice.

'Chesterton was born a liar and a rogue; no doubt he'll die the same, sir. The first time I saw him working in this garden, I knew it. I *knew* it! I've tended the soil for over fifty years, sir, and I know how it should be treated. This man –' he shrugged his shoulders.

'Why, you –' began Chesterton, furiously.

Kennedy, hitherto motionless, stepped forward and gripped the man's arm. Chesterton's veins stood out on his forehead and on his neck, and he bared his teeth.

''Tis true, every word of it,' said Battley, stolidly. 'Any gardener will tell ye so, sir.'

Folly nodded.

'And you didn't offer him the diamonds?'

'Had I known where to find them, I would have handed them back to the family,' said Battley.

'You liar!' roared Chesterton. 'You'd 'and them back, that's a fine one! Ha! Ha! Ha! They was found in your room, see? In your piller!'

Battley said: 'That may be. I did not put them there, nor did I know that they were there.'

Folly turned to Chesterton, his voice deceptively mild.

'You put them there, didn't you? You dug them up from the shrubbery, and tried to plant them on Battley. You were seen, you know. You might as well admit it.'

'No one ever seed me!' Chesterton said sullenly.

'Oh, yes, someone did,' said Folly pleasantly. 'Commander Fayne –'

Chesterton stared, his face gathering to an intensity of fury that even Battley had not as yet called forth.

''Im!' he gasped. ''E told you? 'E *told* you, 'e ratted on me? Why? I'll make 'im –'

'What do you know about him?' asked Folly smoothly, the point of his questioning reached at last.

'What do *I* know about 'im?' muttered Chesterton. 'I know that 'e – '

'I'll allow no lies of one of the family,' Battley shouted angrily.

'Lies!' bellowed Chesterton. 'Lies, that's a fine one. *I* can tell you about that ruddy sailor! 'E – '

Before he had finished what he was going to say, Battley hurled himself on him with such fury that both fell heavily to the ground. Webb and Kennedy sprang forward, but it was Folly who disentangled the fighting men; seizing Battley in an iron grip as Chesterton rolled clear, gasping for breath, his hands clawing at his throat.

Chapter 24

Some of the Truth

Battley, again on his feet, remained silent to all Folly's persuasiveness and cunningly posed questions he turned an unheeding ear.

Clearly, both Battley and Chesterton knew something which would incriminate Charles Fayne. Although Battley was stubborn, Chesterton was aching to tell what he knew, and Folly was making him more impatient with every moment he spent questioning Battley.

Folly stopped at last.

'If you won't talk, you won't,' he said. 'Kennedy – take him outside and put him in one of the cars. Don't leave him.'

Folly turned to Chesterton, his voice, his whole demeanour, one of grave severity.

'You're in for a bad time,' he said. 'You attacked the Inspector, you had possession of stolen diamonds, you feloniously entered private premises. That adds up to something. You'll get seven years if you get a day.'

Chesterton's shifty face settled into lines of whining aggression.

'I never knew 'e was a cop.'

'I might believe that in some circumstances,' said Folly. '*If* I believe you, the charge might be reduced. Now, come on, what do you know? Did you dig those diamonds up?'

'Supposing I did?' muttered Chesterton.

'Never mind supposing. Did you?'

'Yeah.'

'And you were seen by Commander Fayne –'

'I was seen by the Navy, the –' Chesterton broke off and sneered. ''E wanted the sparklers for 'isself. Stole 'em once before, 'e did. Four or five years ago. 'E 'ocked 'em.'

'You mean he pawned them?' demanded Folly.

'Same thing – my guv'nor lent 'im five 'undred quid on

them, see. 'E took 'em out, last week. Paid up for them o' course. But 'arf the notes 'e paid were duds. I come arter the sparklers for me guv'nor who 'ad the tip-orf, see? Said they was buried in the shrubbery.' Chesterton cocked his head, as if to catch in his own voice the correct not of authenticity. 'I 'ad a look round, and found a bit of grass wot 'ad bin dug up. Just as I was looking up comes the Navy. Come near to blinding me, 'e did!'

Folly said: 'I see. So you got away with them, and planted them at Battley's cottage.'

'I was only trying to 'ide the sparklers so's they wouldn't get lorst again.' He stared into Folly's eyes with what he hoped was limpid innocence.

'Now let's get this straight. You knew that Commander Fayne had stolen the diamonds, because, some years ago – '

'My guv'nor knew they'd been stolen – 'e 'appened to 'ear about it. Then the Navy – 'e was in Civvy Street then! – comes and 'ocks them.'

'And your – guv'nor – failed to report that to the police?'

'Supposin' 'e did?' demanded Chesterton truculently. 'E 'ad a n'arrangement with Mr Mottram, so it was all on the square. Mr Mottram wanted 'im to keep the sparklers until they was taken out of 'ock. Soon as they was taken, the guv'nor passed the word to Mr Mottram, see? Last Sunday, 'e told 'im.'

'Sunday!' exclaimed Webb. 'What time?'

'Early arternoon.'

Folly spoke meditatively.

'So now we know why Mottram cancelled his appointment with the solicitor. He called the family together, to tell them that at last he knew all about the diamonds, but something went wrong. He delayed it – '

'An before 'e got any further, the Navy croaked 'im,' added Chesterton obligingly.

'How do you know?' snapped Folly sharply. 'Come on, out with it! How do you *know*?'

Chesterton rocked back on his heels, as one reasoning man to another. 'It stands ter reason, don't it?'

'Is that the best you can do?'

'The minnit I knew that Mr Mottram 'ad been croaked, I saw it plain,' declared Chesterton. 'If you want *proof*, yer'd better arst Battley.'

'Did you see Commander Fayne here on Monday?'

'See 'im Sunday in Listow,' said Chesterton. 'Then I lorst 'im. But someone passed the tip-orf to the guv'nor an' told 'im where the sparklers was.'

Folly said: 'Who told him?'

'You'd better arst 'im,' said Chesterton, slyly.

'Where is he?' demanded Folly.

'In London, somewhere, like I told yer.'

Folly regarded him through narrowed eyes, and then nodded decisively.

'All right! You'll go into Listow for questioning. I'll remember that you've been frank.' He gave the necessary orders.

'Oh, one more thing, Chesterton. Where were you this afternoon?'

Chesterton turned, and there was a wide, triumphant grin on his face.

'Thought you'd got me didn't you?' he retorted. 'Well you 'aven't. I couldn't 'ave croaked old Crow if I were with the vicar all the arternoon, now could I?'

Folly snapped:

'How did you know that Crow had been killed?'

'Now I wonder 'ow I knoo,' said Chesterton, still grinning. 'Lemme see, now! Oh, yerse! The vicar told me. While we was 'aving tea. Anything else you wanter know?'

Folly said: 'Yes, how did you come to know Crow?'

'My guv'nor did a lot of business wiv' 'im,' said Chesterton. 'But if you want Crow's murderer, mister, better arst these people wot was in Listow. 'Ave a word with them!'

Folly stared at him, saying nothing. Chesterton slouched off, under guard, to join Battley in Webb's car. There was a truculent, satisfied air about him.

Charles admitted, airily, that he had lied – and that he had seen Chesterton digging up the necklace. Also, he said, he had returned from Listow by a slow train which had stopped at Pelham Halt, and walked across the fields to the house, entering the grounds near the shrubbery. On seeing Chesterton, he had broken off the branch, believing that a man with a weapon was in a healthier position than a man who was not; but Chesterton had been smart enough to get away.

With Webb and Charles, Folly led the way to the shrubbery to inspect the hiding-place.

'So this is the place, is it?' asked Folly, bending down beside a rhododendron bush. 'Used a trowel, I see – ah, there it is. Hum! Says that someone told his Guv'nor where the necklace was buried. A remarkable story!' To Webb's surprise, Folly told Charles of what Chesterton had said about Battley trying to sell him the necklace.

Charles listened attentively.

'Does it strike you as likely?' Folly asked.

'It might be,' said Charles, a little uncertainly. 'But why ask me?'

'Yours is an opinion that could be worth having,' said Folly, enigmatically. 'I want the truth, you know. Nothing else. You might pass that on to the rest of your relatives, by the way.'

Charles said: 'You haven't done much to convince them.'

'Perhaps we're looking at it from different angles,' suggested Folly, silkily. 'For we're trying to find a murderer, not conceal one.'

Charles smiled, without visible signs of amusement. 'My own position entirely!'

Folly's left lid rose momentarily showing a sharp, intelligent eye.

'I wonder! Still, that's not the point at the moment. About Chesterton and these diamonds – you've told us the whole truth about them?'

'The whole truth and nothing but,' Charles assured him. 'Chesterton is a liar, I hope you realise that?'

'Oh, yes! But he's also loyal to Dering,' said Folly. 'So we can take it that Dering briefed him as to what to say if he were caught.'

'Then Dering instructed him to plant the diamonds on Battley!' cried Webb, triumphant at discovering a point he considered Folly had overlooked.

'That's so,' said Folly unemotionally. 'Battley had always hated them both. Popular theory was that Battley resented being thrown out. Could have been something less obvious. Deep waters everywhere, aren't there, Commander?'

Charles's smile was facile. 'Yes, aren't there.'

'Well, there's nothing more to be got here, better get back to the house.' Folly led the way, without looking at Charles.

'So you went to Crow's shop, and found the door locked?'

'That's so,' said Charles, calmly.

'Why did you want to see Crow?'

'I did a little private detecting,' said Charles, blandly. 'The pictures were stolen from the attic, you know, and I thought perhaps Crow knew something about it.'

'Why should he?' demanded Folly.

'He did some business with my uncle.'

'What made you think that the canvases were your uncle's?' asked Folly, curiously.

'You've probably heard that my uncle fancied himself as an artist,' said Charles. 'His favourite subject was himself.'

'And you had no great regard for him?' murmured Folly.

'I couldn't honestly say that I had,' admitted Charles.

'Nor for his pictures?'

'They were tripe,' Charles was emphatic.

Folly snapped: 'Then why did you go to the trouble of visiting Crow to find out if he had them?'

Charles, smiled genially, extricating himself glibly from the trap.

'I told you that I was doing a little private detecting, Superintendent. I knew that the pictures had been stolen, and I thought the murderer might have taken them. I happen to believe that none of the family had anything to do with killing Silas. I wanted to try to find out just what had been happening.'

Folly shot him a sceptical look.

'*Very* plausible,' he commented, ironically. 'But I don't think you're really being frank with us, sir. Inspector, would you mind going with Commander Fayne into the morning-room? I'll join you there in a minute.'

Charles looked surprised, and Webb smiled secretly, guessing that all Folly wanted was to keep Charles on tenterhooks. As they waited in the little room, Charles began to fill his pipe, which was well alight, then to fidget with ornaments and books. They waited for nearly a quarter of an hour.

When the door opened and Folly came in, all gentle amiability, all signs of conciliation, were gone.

'Ah!' he glared at Charles. 'Well, sir? Have you decided to tell me the truth?'

Charles said, evenly: 'I've told you the truth.'

'Have you? I doubt it!' Folly's voice and demeanour were aggressive. 'Some time ago, sir, there was a theft from this house. Of money and jewels. You doubtless recall the incident?'

'Of course,' said Charles, watching Folly closely.

'You raised money on that necklace!' Folly roared. 'And you redeemed it recently. You brought it here and tried to use it to transfer police attention from yourself to Mrs Fayne. You knew that your uncle had discovered the crime, and you killed him in order to prevent it from being brought home to you! Now, sir – ' he thundered the words – 'deny that if you can!'

Charles, pale-faced, stared at him without speaking.

'Deny it, if you can!' repeated Folly, his voice resonant with accusation. 'You stole the necklace! You tried to persuade your uncle not to tell the others! He refused, and so you murdered him! Then you saw your danger, and tried to implicate Mrs Fayne. You did not work alone, you had an accomplice, a clever accomplice, resident in Pelham.'

Charles said: 'I did not steal the necklace. I did not try to do anything to cast suspicion on Valerie and, I did not kill Uncle Silas.'

Folly brushed the assertions aside.

'You discovered, later, that Crow knew what you had done. You went to reason with him, but he would not heed you, so you killed him also. You found some of the missing canvases but one was left behind. Before you could prise it from his dead fingers, your brother arrived. You hid until he had gone. Then Inspector Webb and I arrived. Webb found the body, but you assaulted him, in a further effort to get the canvas which the dead man was clutching. I know you were there, sir!' Folly drew a deep breath and his eyes were blazing with the veracity of an inborn actor. 'I saw your back view, which I have seen again this evening. Now, sir! Let us have done with this foul lying, this miserable twisting and turning to avoid the consequences of your odious crimes!'

The room was very quiet, and only the sound of breathing disturbed the silence – until Charles uttered a sharp exclamation.

'I did not do it, Folly!'

'And what do you think your word is worth?' demanded

Folly, coldly. 'How much chance do you think you have of being believed by a jury?'

'If you know your job, it won't get as far as that,' Charles retorted.

'Indeed, sir? You must forgive us poor, benighted policemen, we heavy-footed, empty-minded individuals who do not know our own job, who are in great need of advice and guidance from such as yourself. Be advised by me, sir! *A jury would convict you on the evidence I can supply for them.* I have no wish to see an innocent man convicted for a crime he has not done. You claim that you are not the murderer, then give me some evidence in support of your claim, and at the same time explain your earlier lies and behaviour.'

'I've nothing more to say,' said Charles.

'Indeed? In that case, your protestations of innocence do not appear to me to be worth the breath you have used to utter them. Now – ' Folly raised his hands, a human, even an appealing note crept into his voice – 'be reasonable, Commander. You might conceivably be trying to protect someone you like – or whom you love,' he added, unexpectedly.

For the first time, Charles looked taken aback.

'Don't talk nonsense!' he said, roughly.

'Nonsense? Nonsense, is it?' asked Folly, very softly. 'Commander, it distresses me to have to touch upon personal matters, which are close to the heart, but since you have been here I have noticed that you have been at pains to have little to do with your cousin, Lynda. I ask you to believe that I am no fool. In my opinion, there is an understanding between you, and – '

'There is nothing of the kind!' Charles snapped, a little too hastily

'Let me make myself clear,' said Folly in the easy, expansive tone of a man who had only too thoroughly already done so. 'I would have respect for any man who, however mistakenly, tried to protect someone whom he loved from the consequence of a crime. The tragedy would be if he put himself in danger for her sake, when in fact there was no danger for her.'

Webb watched, fascinated. He believed that Charles was about to break down, in some degree at least. Folly had worked with a cunning, a cleverness which marked all he did. Now, if Charles Fayne was in love with Lynda, he must be thinking that by refusing to talk freely, he might increase suspicions against her, instead of ease them.

At last, Charles said, slowly:

'Very well then, I am in love with Lynda. I have been for years. She has done nothing to encourage me. I have no knowledge that she has played any part in this crime. I am concealing nothing from you about her. Is that clear enough?'

Folly looked at him steadily.

'Thank you, Commander! Your information will be treated in strict con –'

The door was flung violently open, admitting Lynda and Robin, with Valerie on their heels. Feldmann and William followed more sedately.

Folly surveyed the group icily.

'What is the meaning of this intrusion?'

Lynda said: 'It wasn't Charles who –'

'You're crazy if you think it was Charles,' Robin cut in. 'This has got to stop, Folly.'

'Indeed?' said Folly, with the awful voice of authority. 'Let me remind you, sir, that the processes of the law do not stop until their full circle has been completed.'

'I protest against this most illegal cross-examination,' boomed William, agitatedly.

Valerie said nothing. She was at a loss because Feldmann had said so little and appeared so insignificant beside Folly.

'I am fully aware of the legal position,' Folly glared stonily at Feldmann. 'Do you wish to make a statement? Or am I to be permitted to continue questioning a member of this household against whom no charge has yet been preferred?'

Feldmann smiled.

'I would like a word with you, Folly, yes,' he said mildly.

'I am the most forbearing of men,' declared Folly, with a heavy sigh very slightly tinged, to the initiated, to Webb, with unease. 'Please proceed.'

'There appears to be some mistake about the reason for my being here,' said Feldmann, and in the pause which followed one could have heard a pin drop. 'Mr William Mottram asked me to come,' went on Feldmann, 'and he has made it clear that he wishes me to act for him. However, at the moment, I see no purpose in acting for him or anyone else – as you have pointed out, no charge has been made, therefore, no one here yet requires legal aid. At most, I am holding a watching brief.'

'Feldmann!' exploded William. 'What –'

Feldmann silenced him with a motion of his hand.

'And I *am* holding a watching brief,' he declared, 'but not for any person present. Silas Mottram was an old friend of mine. He gave me to understand that he was in fear of his life. When I last saw him, he told me he was afraid that one of his relatives might kill him, and charged me not to render any one of them practical assistance during the course of police investigation.'

After a long, tense, pause, Folly's natural voice, small, naked, innocently free from histrionics, exclaimed:

'Good gracious me!'

'Feldmann!' howled William, 'you –'

'If the police should prefer a charge against anyone here, I will be quite free to act,' Feldmann said, 'but until then, I am afraid I can only play the role of spectator. It is obviously time that my position was made quite clear.'

Folly began to smile.

'So Silas hasn't left us,' Robin said, bitterly. 'How far had Folly got, Charles? Was he going to drag you off?'

'Don't ask me,' said Charles.

'They mustn't arrest you,' said Lynda, in a high, almost hysterical voice.

She looked distraught. Webb would have been puzzled by Charles's expression but for his confession of his love for his cousin.

'In spite of both temporary and permanent setbacks,' said Folly heavily, 'I propose to get to the bottom of this wicked business before the day is over. You may have heard my statement to Charles Fayne. I have all the evidence which I require to charge him with murder in the first degree. I propose to –'

'Not *Charles*!' exclaimed Robin.

'You can't!' broke in Lynda. 'It's crazy! You're wrong, hopelessly wrong!'

'Is that so?' asked Folly smoothly. 'Perhaps you can tell me what is right, Miss Mottram?'

'I can –' began Lynda.

'Hold it, old girl,' said Charles. His voice was quiet, but there was warning in it. 'Folly's trying to panic us but we needn't let him succeed.'

Lynda said: 'I'm not going to let him build up a case against you for my sake, and you needn't think I am! Charles did not steal the necklace, Inspector. I did. So he had not got a motive for killing Silas.'

Folly said:

'Not that motive, no. But you had one, Miss Mottram,' he paused, then added: 'Shall we now have the whole truth?'

Chapter 25

More Facts

Lynda spoke composedly, while looking at Charles as if defying him to interrupt.

Valerie was not alone in believing that she was hearing some part of the truth at last. Robin looked as if he knew it all already, and William, sadly deflated, sat staring stonily ahead.

'I'll tell you the truth as far as I know it,' said Lynda, 'and I'll start off with the necklace. I took it, five years ago. I was desperately hard-up, and wanted to borrow five hundred pounds, but neither William nor Uncle Silas would let me have it. I was in debt and being served with writs – I knew it would ruin my credit everywhere if I allowed the things to reach court. So, when the others were together, I took the necklace.'

She paused, and Folly nodded.

'Charles found out,' said Lynda. 'We travelled back together, and he kept on at me until I admitted it. He – ' she smiled at Charles, warmly – 'he agreed with my reasoning – that it was a family piece, held in trust by Uncle Silas, but it was mine as much as it was his. The police weren't likely to agree, but morally I was right. Charles wouldn't let me try to sell it – he took it, raised money on it, and sent me the money – just over five hundred pounds. It saw me through. Both of us hoped that before long one of us would be in a position to take it out of pawn, but it wasn't possible, until a few days ago.'

She looked at Folly for the first time.

'I see,' said Folly, mildly. 'What happened when it was redeemed?'

Charles spoke quietly.

'You may as well have the whole story, I suppose. Lynda's right, that's exactly what happened, except that I didn't actually pawn it – I borrowed the money from an acquaintance. I thought it would be better if I did it that way. To get it back, I've been putting a bit aside for years, but it takes a long time to save five hundred pounds, and I made matters a lot worse by plunging on the races in the hope of winning a lump sum and getting the thing off our minds. Instead, I got further into debt. In the end I borrowed enough to bring my savings up to the required amount, and got the necklace back.'

'Assuming that you are telling the truth, Commander, and I must admit that I think you are, what happened to the necklace?' asked Folly. 'You have not forgotten, I hope, that it was placed on the doorstep of this house, and that afterwards Inspector Webb was assaulted and the necklace again stolen?'

'I didn't knock him on the head,' Charles said, with a grin. 'Nor did I put it in the porch – it isn't as straightforward as that.' He looked light-heartedly at Folly. 'I came down on Sunday, as you know, to see Silas, bringing the necklace with me. I'd gathered that all of us would be seeing him – he was at the Cross Inn, by the way, a pub a couple of miles outside Pelham. I thought I could tuck the case in the side of a chair, where he couldn't miss it, and he'd be none the wiser about who brought the diamonds back. He was very much on edge, and hustled me out pretty quickly, but I managed to leave the necklace as I'd planned – and that was the last I saw of it until Chesterton dug it out of the ground this afternoon.'

'Were you the first of the relatives to see your uncle?' asked Folly.

'I think so.'

'From whom did you borrow the money on the diamonds?'

'Didn't I tell you?' Charles looked surprised. 'It was Dering.'

'Dering!' exclaimed Folly. 'And you repaid him recently?'

'About a week ago,' said Charles, 'and he was in excellent health I assure you. I had no idea he was a crony of my uncle's.'

Folly looked disapprovingly at his small, bright toes.

'I should have known of this much earlier, but I suppose I must credit you with good motives, even if mistaken ones.

Can't you say for sure whether you were the first to visit your uncle at this country inn?'

'No,' said Charles, 'but I think I was. No one else was mentioned.'

'He was the first,' said Lynda. 'I came just after him, and had the same reception. Silas telephoned Robin, to postpone his appointment, and went in to Listow to meet William. Yes, you're quite right,' she added with a touch of bitterness. 'Both William and I had the chance of taking the necklace again. I didn't take it, and I don't think that William – '

'I had no idea at all that it had been returned!' exclaimed William, 'not the *faintest* idea!'

'Someone else could have taken it,' said Folly, soothingly. 'Someone else, who visited your uncle at the Cross. Has anyone any idea?'

'Dering saw Silas in Listow,' said Lynda, slowly. 'I know, because I followed him. Silas went to Crow's shop, and Dering followed him. I think that uncle's disquiet was caused by Dering – it was Dering who lent the money on the necklace, wasn't it, Charles?'

'Yes,' said Charles.

'Were your uncle and Dering acquainted then?'

'Yes – because of their interest in pictures,' said Charles. 'Dering was an undercover dealer in pictures, precious stones and antiques. I knew that he would keep the necklace for me, all right – I'd met him once or twice, as I'm interested in old paintings myself. I didn't think for a moment that he knew Uncle Silas well enough to confide in him.'

'I see,' said Folly ponderously. 'I see. We will return to Dering shortly. Meanwhile Commander, tell me, why did you go into Listow today and why did you lie to me about finding Crow's shop door locked?'

Charles said: 'I knew that if you discovered I'd had the handling of the necklace, you'd accept it as a motive for murder. I believed that the pictures, not the diamonds, were the real motive, and I thought Crow might know something about them. They were Uncle Silas's pictures – he left them here himself, and I believe, he came here once or twice to paint in the attic. He and Dering were on good terms, as I'd discovered, and he visited The Paddocks from time to time.' Charles paused, choosing his words carefully. 'When I got to the shop, the door was open. Crow was dead, I found the canvases but hadn't been there more than two minutes before Robin arrived. He saw Crow and hurried out again. Then Webb arrived. I threw a cloth over his head, while I tried to get the last canvas from Crow. Then someone started creating a disturbance at the shop door, so I gave it up and cut for cover.'

'I see,' said Folly, heavily. 'Why were you so anxious to get those canvases?'

'I've told you. I thought they held the secret of the first murder.'

'But surely you would have been wise to have informed Inspector Webb or myself?'

Charles raised his eyebrows. 'I don't think so! First of all, I was worried because of the necklace business, which might be brought home to Lynda.' He shrugged. 'Then, before that was settled I'd been in Crow's shop when he was dead. I decided that I'd better lie myself out of it.'

'What did you do with the canvases?'

'I left them at Listow Station,' said Charles, putting his hand to his pocket and taking out a slip of paper. 'There's the cloakroom ticket.'

Folly reached for it, nodded, and then turned to Robin:

'Why did you go to Mr Crow's shop, Mr Fayne?'

Robin spoke equably; Valerie sensed a great change in him, as if a heavy load had been lifted from his mind.

'I was on the same stunt as Charles,' he said.

'And am I to assume that your earlier evasions were prompted by the same motives?'

'They were,' said Robin. 'I'll fill in a few details if you like.'

'Please do,' said Folly grimly.

Robin glanced at Valerie, and there was a warmth in his smile which made her heart leap.

'I knew about the necklace and I was fairly sure who had taken it. I didn't know what part Charles had played but –' he looked apologetically at Charles. 'I was afraid he'd killed Silas!'

'You ass!' said Charles, smiling broadly.

'You see, Charles was here on Monday night,' said Robin. 'Valerie had gone to bed early, and Charles tapped at my window. We went into the whole business pretty thoroughly before he left. Silas was *not* here – not to my knowledge, at all accounts. I was anxious not to embroil Valerie in the old family scandal, so I said nothing about it.

Then Charles wired me at my office, asking to meet me at Chester, and I thought he was probably making an alibi for himself. We acted pretty well, and we didn't let anyone know we'd met earlier. I don't think anyone we met at the hotels would have guessed differently.'

'Why did you consider such acting necessary if you knew nothing of the murder?' inquired Folly.

Robin grinned. 'But I did know of the murder – Charles had telephoned.'

'Then be good enough to say why you acted so furtively, on Monday night,' said Folly at last.

'We didn't mean to let Silas know that we both knew Lynda had borrowed the necklace,' said Robin. 'The trouble is, Folly, that you'll never be able to understand how we felt about Silas. Whenever we had a chance to put one over him, we took it. It was the only thing that made him bearable. A year ago, I had a fierce quarrel with him about the necklace which he accused me of taking. We patched up the quarrel later, but it was always in our minds, at least, it was in mine. I decided to have nothing more to do with him, if it could possibly be avoided. However, I met him at the club by chance, and he told me that The Paddocks was empty. I made an offer for it, right away. He didn't ask any questions, and I didn't volunteer any information. Had he known I was marrying, he would have said "no", out of sheer cussedness. He didn't reduce the rent at all, but we had an agreement for seven years made out and signed – Feldmann drew it up. I thought, in time, everything would settle down,' said Robin, reasonably. 'Instead, Silas got on the warpath and called this meeting. Remember, he was capable of cutting any one of us out of his will.' Robin shrugged. 'Had it been his own money, I would have told him to go to the devil with it! But it was mostly inherited, and we had some right to it. I think we all felt the same. That was why we agreed to meet him.'

Robin paused. The silence was broken unexpectedly by Feldmann. He gave a little, preliminary cough.

'I know why Mr Mottram wished to see them,' he said. 'He had told me that he would see them on the Monday – but apparently he preferred to cut my appointment without informing me, so as to see them on the Sunday.'

'Well?' barked Folly. 'Why?'

'He was afraid of being murdered,' said Feldmann, softly.

'He suspected one or all of the family. He proposed to bring it into the open, and to accuse them while they were all together, hoping to set one off against the other. That is all he wanted.'

'Why had he made his appointment with you?' asked Folly, sharply.

Feldmann smiled.

'For a very simple reason. He proposed to reach his own conclusion as to which members of the family hated him enough to kill him, and cut them out of his will. The will, some ten years old – after a few minor bequests, leaves the whole estate divided equally amongst the cousins,' said Feldmann. 'It is a considerable fortune. After payment of death duties, it will amount to something more than half a million pounds.'

Charles stared at him, his lips parted.

'Half a *million*!' gasped Lynda.

'Are you *sure*?' demanded William, hoarsely.

'I am quite sure,' said Feldmann, dryly.

'Well, well!' said Robin, 'it was less than a hundred thousand when he inherited. May we know how he has increased it?'

'That would be an interesting problem for the family, no doubt,' said Folly, 'but it hardly affects the present situation. The first fact does. The prospect of inheriting so large a fortune as one fourth of half a million pounds might induce many people to commit murder. Many people,' he repeated, gently, 'and while we have been given plausible explanations of much that has happened, we have *not* yet found who murdered Silas Mottram and Crow.'

Chapter 26

The Discovery in the Church

Folly did not stress the obvious, but used his favourite method of leading up to a point when the position became almost intolerable, and then leaving everybody in a nerve-racking suspense. He then shut himself in a room with Webb and the telephone.

Actually, he telephoned Scotland Yard and asked them to make a wide search for Dering. That done he replaced the receiver and grinned at Webb.

'How are you feeling, Inspector?'

'I suppose part of it is true,' said Webb, cautiously.

'You mean you're pulled two ways – you like young Fayne, but you aren't satisfied that he's been really frank? Poor chap!'

Webb stared. 'What the dickens are you getting at now?'

'Nothing remarkable in that, surely,' said Folly, virtuously. 'Wouldn't you be sorry for yourself if you were in love, but hadn't a chance in a thousand?'

'I'm not sure about that chance in a thousand,' said Webb, speculatively, 'she looked as if she weren't altogether unaware of his attractions.'

Folly frowned. 'So you noticed that, too, did you?'

'I thought Robin's story of meeting his brother furtively was rather weak,' said Webb, adding thrust to thrust.

'And so it was! He told the truth as far as it goes, I think – which is probably not far. Another curious thing,' Folly added, 'is this enormous fortune. Has Mottram been up to something, I wonder?'

'We'll have to try to find that out,' said Webb, a little dispiritedly.

Folly looked at him shrewdly. 'Food, Webb! That is the answer. These hours, how many – one, two, three, four? – unsustained, well nigh famished, must come to an end! We must call a halt! Vol-au-vent of pike quenelles and mushrooms, baked potatoes in their jackets! Of what joys, what necessities, are we being deprived! By the way, who will be left here to keep an eye on things?'

'Bennett and Kennedy,' said Webb, 'and a constable.'

'They'll have to do,' said Folly, walking rapidly, almost running, through The Paddocks to his car, Webb panting at his heels.

The family seeing him go so speedily, was a little mystified. Nervously visualising new clues to be unearthed, further ordeals by questioning. They avoided looking at each other. Only Valerie was happy, believing in Robin's explanation. William seemed to suffer from the strain more than the others. Affability sat uneasily upon him; he would have been more natural had he been solemn and resentful.

At dinner they spoke determinedly of Silas's surprising fortune, but gradually this determination eroded, worn down by persistent underlying anxiety, they found themselves openly discussing the implications of Folly's decision to leave the house.

'Don't let him deceive you,' said Feldmann. 'While all of you may be quite satisfied with your own motives for concealing relevant facts, the police are certainly not going to rest content.'

Charles grinned.

'What I like about you, sir, is your cheerful optimism. The point has been taken!'

Words, sombre or gay, passed over Valerie's head. She was surprised at the family's irresponsible reference to the necklace, the casually careful substitution of the word 'borrowed' for the more realistic one of 'theft'. This example of family unity she found both touching in its loyalty, and shocking in its bland dishonesty.

'I wonder what Folly phoned about?' Robin said, towards the end of the meal.

'That's what he wants us to wonder,' declared Charles.

'Find Dering, and you will find the murderer,' declared William, looking around him challengingly. 'I have little doubt that the whole problem will be solved when Dering is detained and questioned.'

Charles looked at him, smiling sardonically.

'That would be a comfortable solution, popular with everyone. Excepting Dering, of course.'

'But my dear fellow,' boomed William, 'Dering and his

man Chesterton are very deeply involved. It is evident that Uncle Silas discovered the threat came from Dering, not from one of us. Thus he did not trouble to keep his appointment with you, Percy, because he had no reason to alter his will. We need worry no more!'

'The oracle has spoken!' exclaimed Charles, good-humouredly. 'Well, I'm going to bed!'

The others also went up early.

As Valerie, happy, now, in her renewed trust in Robin – opened her bedroom door, a figure rose from the chair at the foot of her bed, startled, she exclaimed aloud.

'What's the trouble?' asked Robin, quickly.

'Sorry if I scared you.' Charles stood there, tall and still. 'There's something I wanted to say – ' he glanced meaningly at Robin as he broke off.

Valerie's heart missed a beat. 'Haven't I heard everything?' she demanded.

'What has he told you?' asked Charles, carefully.

'*Is* there anything else?' demanded Valerie, looking from one to the other uncertainly. 'Don't keep me waiting, I can't stand much more of it.'

Robin squeezed her arm.

'There's nothing serious,' he assured her, 'I was going to tell you immediately we got up here. The thing is – ' he sat on the edge of the bed, as Valerie sank on to the dressing-table stool – 'that Charles and I weren't moved only by curiosity when we went to see Crow about those pictures. Whether we should have told the police the real reason – ' he paused.

Valerie said, emphatically:

'If you're still holding something back, you're both bigger fools than I thought you were!'

Charles chuckled.

'Blunt and to the point. The thing is, Val, if Robin and I are right, we've un-cupboarded a somewhat embarrassing family skeleton.'

'Aren't they all?' said Valerie bitterly. 'What extra quality of embarrassment does this one hold?'

Robin said soberly:

'Silas's extraordinary rise in fortune. The point is, that Charles, by chance, heard from a friend of his, that a Gainsborough had been stolen. Later, calling on Silas unexpectedly, he *thought* he recognised it in a picture Silas was examining. Silas covered it up almost at once, but afterwards Charles began to brood. There's a big market abroad, and here, for stolen or faked old masters. It could be that the pictures in the attic had been painted over – '

Valerie drew a deep breath.

'Haven't you got *any* sense? Don't you see what it might mean?'

Robin said: 'Yes, we do! Personally, I doubted it because I thought the new paint might spoil the old – '

Charles interrupted him, and neither of them seemed aware that Valerie was staring at each in turn, with a growing feeling of exasperation and alarm.

'Not if it were done skilfully. I've come to the conclusion that Silas and Dering were in it together – Dering would know why he chose to come here to do the work. I mean, if it weren't something pretty hot, why should Silas come from London? I wouldn't be surprised if Dering helped to dispose of the things, and Crow had something to do with it. Do you know what I think?'

'I do know that you ought to tell the police, right away,' said Valerie.

'And put the name of Silas Mottram to shame for ever?' asked Robin, lightly.

Valerie swung round on him.

'You and your precious family name! Haven't you an ounce of common sense between you? Don't you realise what the police will think if they learn this for themselves? If they catch Dering, they'll find out about it, and then – '

Robin looked startled.

'It didn't strike me that – '

'You're so wrapped up in the family that you don't let yourself think!' said Valerie, fiercely.

Charles regarded her with a one-sided smile.

'No, let the police find this out for themselves, if its going to be found out, enough of our dirty linen is already being washed in public. I was going to say,' he went on as Valerie simmered, unable to trust herself to speak, 'that we knew Silas did some business with Crow, and thought we'd have a look round,' said Charles. 'Incidentally,' he went on, with a show of nonchalance, 'we didn't tell each other where we were going, it was arranged independently.'

'And you walked into a trap!' exclaimed Valerie.

'Well, we couldn't help that,' said Charles.

Valerie drew in her breath.

'You're hopeless, both of you! I –'

'Give us a hearing,' pleaded Charles. 'The real meat of our theory is to come – that Silas and Dering were working together, that Crow discovered that they were in this crooked business, that Dering decided to kill Silas for his own safety, and then to kill Crow to make doubly sure. Pretty good, don't you think?'

'What good will it do if we advance that theory to the police?' Robin demanded, judicially. 'They'll think we're hatching it up to distract their attention from ourselves.'

Valerie looked from one to the other, and spoke with studied calm.

'If you were ten years old, each of you, what nice, ingenious little boys you'd make! But you're grown men!' She saw that this time she really had pierced their good-humoured tolerance of her, and went on fiercely:

'I don't want to sound like a gramophone record, but you must tell Webb or Folly, and you mustn't delay another minute.'

'But *why?*' demanded Robin, clinging to his theory with masculine obstinacy.

'Because if they find out that these pictures are painted over real ones – valuable ones – which have been stolen, do you seriously think they'll believe that you went to get the canvases just to find out the truth about Silas?' Valerie insisted. 'Of course they won't! They'll think that you meant to get hold of those pictures for yourselves at all costs. It will be a motive for killing both Silas and Crow – and you aren't clear of either murder yet!'

Charles said slowly, 'I hadn't seen it that way.'

'It's so glaringly obvious!' cried Valerie. 'Even now, you'll find it hard to explain why you didn't tell them before. Let's go downstairs and ring them up right away.' She stood up and went to the door, determinedly.

After a pause, the two men followed her, subdued, a little outraged at having their plot snatched from them. They went downstairs together, Valerie on edge to get to the telephone, seeing so much more clearly than either of them the danger in which they stood.

The incredible thing was that they had not realised it for themselves.

Before returning to Listow, Folly and Webb called at the Vicarage.

Frend greeted them courteously, but Folly came to the point with grave directness, demanding how Frend had come to know about Crow's murder.

Frend answered with engaging promptness.

'Symes, the reporter of the local paper told me. He rang me up, as he does every week, before his paper went to Press. I gave him parish details – Pelham has a regular column in the paper, you see. He mentioned it because he knew that I knew Crow.'

'And Chesterton was with you for some time this afternoon?'

'He was,' said Frend.

'What was he doing here?'

'Why are people found at vicarages?' asked Frend, his gaunt face thoughtful. 'I think I had better be quite frank now, even in giving opinions. Chesterton was never popular in Pelham, but now and again, when he was living here, he came to church. And once or twice, I found him in church, by himself, praying.' Frend's eyes, for a moment, were those of a visionary. 'In view of that, I thought I might be able to help him. When I saw him in the church this afternoon, I naturally invited him into the vicarage. He was here when Symes phoned me.'

'So that's it,' mused Folly. 'Very simple, after all, except – do you seriously think he wanted spiritual guidance, Mr Frend?'

'If I were asked for my opinion, as a man, I would say that it is unlikely,' said Frend. 'But I am a minister of the gospel, and I have known of many remarkable conversions. I thought that Chesterton, in a tongue-tied, embarrassed fashion, was trying to find something which he knew he lacked, but needed. I did all that I could to help him.'

'Did he give you the same impression this afternoon?' asked Folly, curiously.

'I can't say that he did,' Frend admitted. 'This is a most difficult situation for me, you understand. How much was I justified in telling you of a man who might have come to me for spiritual guidance?'

Folly said, quietly:

'I think you know where to draw the line, Vicar.'

Frend was silent for some seconds. Then he appeared to

come to a decision. 'All right, Superintendent! When I saw Chesterton today, I thought it was on one of his usual visits, and brought him to the house. You'll forgive me if I say that I really have tried hard with him. At times, I appeared to make some progress, but before he left this afternoon, I missed a silver dish from the tea-table. It was in his pocket.'

Folly leaned forward in his chair.

'I appreciate what you have told me. It doesn't contribute materially to what I already know – that Chesterton is a rogue.' He stared at Frend, his eyelids drooping so that he looked half asleep. After a long pause, he went on: 'Do you remember where you found Chesterton in the church?'

'In one of the pews,' said Frend, reminiscently.

'In any particular one?'

Frend said carefully:

'Ye-es. Superintendent, what are you implying?'

'Sorry, vicar. Not nice, I know. But I have known churches used for hiding-places. Chesterton might have used yours – in collaboration with somebody else. Will you show us where you found him this afternoon?'

Slowly, Frend stood up, leading the way.

It was nearly dark when they reached the church, the beam of Folly's torch casting a bright glow about the polished pews and the red hassocks. The silence, the utter quietude, seemed to affect them all. Frend led the way, hesitated, and then said:

'It was one of these three pews, I think.'

Folly shone the torch along the hassocks and the strip of carpet lying on the stone floor. Then he moved the torch again, so that it shone more fully on to the hassocks. His voice grew sharp.

'These the ones Dering gave you?'

'Yes, Mr Dering presented us with them, about a year ago. He had fifty made, and so that they could be cleaned, he had them made as loose covers.'

'Loose covers!' breathed Folly, 'I've been blind! I want the covers off these three rows, do you mind?'

It was Webb, who, pulling off a cover, uttered a sharp exclamation which made Folly straighten up and swing the torch towards him.

Something more than a worn-out hassock came into view,

for Webb drew out a black, morroco leather case. The case which had held the diamond necklace.

'We're getting on, Webb!' said Folly cautiously, as they drove away from the Vicarage.

'You'll see Chesterton now, I suppose?'

'No, not yet,' said Folly. 'Let him simmer a while. We've got a country-wide call out for Dering, and he'll show up soon, *if* he's alive.'

'Do you think he's dead?' asked Webb.

'Could be. Deep doings, as I've said before. The members of the Mottram family aren't out of the wood yet, you know. If one of them killed Silas, he might also have killed Dering. There is a cunning, crafty, and clever mind at work here. But I think we've got rid of the side issues. Family honour and a diamond necklace can make a pretty effective screen. Main motive now seems to be the canvases. Might be a lot more than they appear to be. There's a profitable market, here and overseas.'

'For second-rate daubs?' asked Webb.

Folly looked at him speculatively, deciding how to give instruction in its least resented form.

'Anyone can paint over a valuable picture,' he said casually, 'and successfully hide it. A good restorer could get the paint off without damaging the original. Favourite way of hiding valuable pictures. Well, Crow had started work on the canvas he had in his hand, I thought we might find out whether there's another picture beneath it.'

'Can we do it?' demanded Webb. Innocently swallowing the powder with the jam.

'The National Gallery has a laboratory and X-ray apparatus which can pick it out without any trouble,' said Folly. 'Remarkable apparatus – I've seen it at work. So I'm going to leave you, first thing in the morning. I'll be back by tomorrow night. Think you can face it?'

Webb smiled. 'What do you want me to do?'

'Just wait and watch,' said Folly. 'Just wait and watch. We're on to something big, and I think we've found what it is.'

They were about to leave for Webb's home when the telephone rang.

It was Robin Fayne. Folly picked up an extension telephone, and together he and Webb listened to the long, carefully prompted exposition.

At the end of it Folly put down his receiver with the gentleness of one who had almost reached his goal. 'Excellent!' he murmured, reverently. 'Excellent! Just what I was waiting for.'

At The Paddocks, Valerie was by no means satisfied that Webb had accepted the new theory about the pictures as unquestioningly as he had pretended, but Robin and Charles seemed satisfied. As Charles turned to go to his room, however, two doors opened on the landing as if by clockwork, and William and Lynda appeared in their doorways.

'I trust you have not been discussing this matter without giving all of us an opportunity to express our views,' said William.

Lynda, looked searchingly at the three faces, which bore the exposed, peaceful expression of those who had made a clean breast of it.

'We must share and share alike,' she said lightly. 'Have you been up to anything?'

Robin and Charles lost a little of their exaltation, and Valerie spoke for them.

'Yes – Robin and Charles have a theory, and we've passed it on to the police.'

'You – you've done *what?*' gasped William.

'We've passed it on to the police,' repeated Valerie coldly. Before he could interrupt again, she repeated what had been said over the telephone so that there could be no mistake about it. Lynda smiled faintly, William seemed on the verge of apoplexy. 'As none of you seem to realise that your necks are in danger, I decided that it was time we worked with the police,' Valerie said, finally. 'If we don't, we can't expect anything but suspicion and embarrassment.'

It was outrageous, William thundered. It was most blameworthy even to have whispered such suspicions of Silas. True, Silas had never treated them as well as he might have done, but that was no excuse for this suspicion. To befoul his memory was a vicious thing. If the suspicions had come unbidden to their minds, they should have kept them to themselves, and certainly before acquainting the police they should have consulted the family. There was now no telling what absurd theories the police might evolve.

'Oh, shut up, William!' said Lynda wearily. 'It can't be undone, and they were probably right anyway.'

'I consider it most reprehensible on Valerie's part to have encouraged this,' snapped William. 'I should have thought that even Valerie would have appreciated the need for keeping the family reputation *unsullied*.'

Robin's eyes glinted.

'We've heard enough from you,' he said, forcefully. 'Val was right. We – '

'That is insolence,' William boomed, cutting off Robin's words by mere volume of sound.

'Easy, folk!' said Charles. 'We don't want to start another feud! If Silas wasn't a crooked dealer in pictures, so much the better. If he was, then the sooner everything's cleared up the sooner this spot of trouble will be over.'

Between them, they pacified William, who returned grumbling to his room. The others settled down, but Robin lay awake for a long time.

Once or twice, he thought he heard movements outside, but decided they were probably imaginary. He turned restlessly from one side to the other. His earlier buoyancy had gone. Valerie had made him realise that there remained a powerful motive for one of them to have killed Silas; the police would not sit back because they had cleared up part of the mystery.

Valerie had been right from the start.

He switched on the dim bedside light, and looked at her. She stirred in her sleep, but did not wake. Sleep erased the lines of anxiety and strain which had been present during the day, and she looked youthful and very lovely.

Robin smiled, sombrely, then abruptly switched off the light. Soon, he fell asleep.

Chapter 27

The Missing Mr Dering

Webb and Folly were up early, Webb a good deal earlier than Folly, for the rhapsodic soliloquy of eggs a la Mornay and creamed haddock scallops, delivered in a gentle – but not too gentle – demanding murmur the evening before, had gnawed into his night's rest. Mrs Webb, however, that dauntless woman, had served kippers without turning a hair, and Folly, humbly and ecstatically, had eaten them. Now a happy, a replete Folly, memories of Dundee marmalade thick cut faintly lingering, waved to Webb from a retreating train.

'It won't be long, now, Webb, we'll get it all sorted out. Have a guessing game while I'm gone!'

'I'll wait till you're back,' retorted Webb.

He decided not to visit The Paddocks, but to let the cousins spend the day in suspense.

There was no news of Dering.

In spite of that, there were so many matters of detail to attend to, that the day passed speedily. By evening, however, he became impatient for news. Had any other Yard man but Folly got through with flying colours, Webb would have expected him to telephone; but Folly would always be unpredictable.

He returned just after ten o'clock, carrying the parcel of canvases.

One swift look, and without a word Webb drew up the largest, the most comfortable chair, a chair already bearing the halo of spiritual dedication, the unmistakable mark of physical pressure. He turned his back as a disconsolate Folly slumped into it, busying himself with an electric hot-plate, cunningly lifting the lid of the coffee pot to allow the healing odour to trail Folly-wards.

'I was wrong!' came Folly's deeply-injured voice. 'Made a damn fool of myself. Nothing behind the daubs – just daubs, that's all, no deep secrets hidden. Wasted a day, had a lousy journey. And there's no news of Dering,' Folly added, as Webb, nipping from saucepan to saucepan, prodded here and spooned there, concocting a panacea to soothe a tired man's wounded pride.

'I looked in at the Yard, they're doing all they can but he's not even been traced to London. Nothing's turned up down here?'

'No,' said Webb, putting a plate down in front of him.

'Beginning to look as though we ought to be searching for his body,' growled Folly. Turning away, turning back, and allowing a fork to be thrust in a not too diffident hand. 'Truth is Webb,' he went on, 'I thought I'd be back with the case all sewn up, now I'm beginning to wonder if we've got the wrong angle.'

'We know a lot we didn't know before,' Webb pointed out, gently pouring.

'Yes. Small consolation. Silas is troubling me, from the grave. Those instructions to Feldmann – he felt pretty sure he was going to be bumped off. The hand from the dead.' He slumped in his chair, then his fingers tightened on the fork. He leaned forward and patted Webb on the arm. 'You're a good fellow Webb. A giver of life. Rare.'

Webb said, slowly:

'As a matter of fact, I've just remembered something which I ought to have thought of before. You've had no luck with your pictures, but there are two which Mrs Fayne moved from the attic. She said it was because they happened to be like Silas Mottram, but she'd never seen Silas.'

Folly, eating slowly, but with growing appreciation, looked up.

'Oh-ho! We certainly ought to have thought of that.' He grew noticeably more cheerful. 'Not your fault, any more than mine. You told me about the two daubs Mrs Fayne kept back, but I forgot 'em too. Careless of us both. Might be the very ones we're after. Still, phone Bennett to say we're on our way.' After Webb had put in the number, he said in a small voice: 'I was laughed at at the National Gallery. Went in full of bounce and bluster, and they laughed at me.'

Webb grinned. 'Too bad!' he said, passing a refilled coffee cup. 'I suppose we haven't taken the wrong turning from the start?'

'I wonder.' Folly's eyes shone. 'It wouldn't surprise me, nothing would, in this case. What's the matter, dear boy, can't you get the number?'

Webb called the exchange again, and was promised a call back. As they stood in the small study, staring at each other, the minutes dragged by, intolerably. Webb was about to press the receiver up and down again, when the operator came through.

'I'm sorry, sir. There's something the matter with the line, I'm afraid. The number doesn't answer. It was all right an hour or two ago, so if you think there should be someone there – '

'There should be, yes,' said Webb, urgently. 'Keep ringing the number and put the call through for the police station if you can get it.'

He replaced the receiver. By then, Folly was halfway to the front door.

'We needn't panic,' said Webb, his own voice unnaturally high, as he got the car out. 'We didn't leave the house unwatched, and my fellows will make sure there's no serious trouble.'

'If that line's been cut, your men might have been knocked over the head,' said Folly, and added unkindly: 'Knocks on the head aren't unknown in this case, are they? Can't you go any faster?'

Webb drove as fast as he dared, but the journey seemed a long one. Every time the car slowed down to take a corner, Folly wailed in protest, leaning forward in his seat, tapping Webb maddeningly on the shoulder.

It had been a trying day at The Paddocks.

William had been unbearable. He moaned about the urgent work awaiting his return to town, he berated Feldmann, and for the first time reproached Lynda for the original 'borrowing' of the diamonds.

The chief trouble was that they expected to see Webb or Folly at any moment, and as the hours passed, they found the suspense increasingly hard to bear.

In relief at the long day drawing to an end at last, they retired early to their rooms.

Valerie fell asleep almost at once.

She was awakened by a crash – startled, sitting up suddenly in bed, she saw that Robin had been awakened too.

Together, tensely, they listened.

A second crash, from above their heads, made Robin fling back the clothes.

'The attic!' he exclaimed.

He jumped out of bed and ran to the door. Other doors opened, and Valerie heard Lynda's voice, then Charles's, and, less clearly, William's, as the men rushed to the attic stairs.

One of the policemen came running up the main flight as Charles reached the attic two or three yards ahead of Robin.

William was standing in the middle of the room, with the light on, and the window wide open. He pointed dramatically to the open window.

'That way – he went out there!'

'Who?' snapped Charles.

'I don't know! Some marauder with no right here! I heard a banging and came up, but the door was locked. I broke it down. Charles! After him, quickly!'

'Get downstairs!' Charles ordered sharply. 'Have the police watch the windows, Robin!'

He went to the attic window and peered out. The moon was rising, and the grounds were bathed in a soft, grey light.

A man was clinging to a sill on the floor below, so closely that he was hardly visible from the attic. Two policemen called up to him, their voices travelling clearly.

Robin and William made their way downstairs.

The hanging figure did not move.

Charles followed in Robin's wake to the next floor. The window immediately beneath the attic was in Lynda's room, but neither Valerie nor Lynda was in sight. Charles flung back the curtains. The light was good enough to reveal the man, caught up in the thick ivy which covered the wall. His face was turned towards the room, his mouth wide open, his eyes staring.

There was an ugly gash under his chin.

Charles muttered: 'Dering!'

He called down to the police. A ladder was run up against the wall and gently easing, the body was dragged into Lynda's room. Dering's eyes stared sightlessly, as they raised him between them and carried him to the bed.

Charles grunted as he straightened up.

'I hope to heaven this is the end of it!'

'What the devil was he doing here?' demanded Robin.

There was constraint between them as they looked at Dering, now covered as far as his shoulders with a blanket.

It seemed fairly obvious that he had fallen from the attic window, jerked his chin against a nail sticking from the wall, and broken his neck. In his pockets were a hack-saw and two blades, a sharp knife, and a roll of silk, generally used for wrapping canvases.

Two further shocks followed, although after the rush of events, neither made so great an impression as the discovery of the body.

The two pictures which Valerie had taken from the attic and put in the sitting-room had gone; cut from their frames. A routine search discovered them below the attic window, fallen from Dering's grasp.

Despatched to telephone headquarters, Bennett, confused, and out of his depth, returned to say the line had been cut.

'Telephone from village,' ordered Kennedy, delighting in this second chance to show authority once again, the splendid powers of deduction they had so pig-headedly overlooked. 'Tell the Superintendent the hunt is over. I have found Dering. You may add, that he came back for the pictures.'

'Quite so, quite so,' said William, his fright and uneasiness vanishing at this neat solution. 'Astonishing! To come back here – remarkable! I wish –'

He stopped at the sound of a car, changing gear, and turning into the drive. None of them expected, or, in fact wished, to see Webb and Folly, but the two men entered the hall together.

'If I may explain, sir –' began Kennedy.

'You can explain how the telephone wire was cut when you were supposed to be watching the house!' snapped Folly, unsympathetically. 'Well, go on. What happened?'

Feldmann, who had joined them after the discovery of Dering's body, cleared his throat with a little preliminary cough.

'It is quite simple, Folly. Dering obviously returned for the pictures, which Mrs Fayne had put in the sitting-room. He took them upstairs, after cutting them out of their frames, and was disturbed by Mr Mottram. In his anxiety to get away, he fell out of the window.'

Folly grunted. 'Where is he? And where *was* he?' As they all started to move, he snapped: 'Mr Fayne – will you come with me? And you, Bennett. I'd like the rest of you to wait here.'

Obeying orders, thought Valerie wearily as she joined the rather huddled group quelled by authority, is becoming part of me.

Upstairs Folly inspected the body, the tools, the canvases, and the nail on which Dering had been caught. Robin found the long silence almost unbearable, but Folly broke it at last, with a sharp mirthless laugh.

'Exquisite!' he observed with parodied admiration. 'Murderer comes back, all the evidence of guilt neatly packed in his pocket. The saw, proving he sawed off the handle of the knife which killed Silas Mottram. The canvases below him – proving it was he who was after the canvases, inferring that he killed Crow to get them. Perfect – perfect!' The cutting edge of his voice pierced all who heard him. 'A beautiful setting – only don't believe it! If he were clever enough to have done all that has been done, he would have been clever enough not to have brought such incriminating things with him tonight. Besides – the pictures were cut out of the frames *downstairs*. If he'd wanted the pictures, having got them, he'd have gone out the way he came in – only he didn't come in!'

'What?' gasped Robin.

'Not without help,' added Folly, his anger slowly subsiding under the benign influence of an attentive audience. 'Police have been watching the house – they wouldn't be likely to miss the doors and ground floor windows. Someone let him in. Found outside Miss Mottram's window, was he? This room?' Robin nodded, hardly able to speak. 'Someone let him in,' Folly repeated. 'Probably the someone who cut the pictures out. Same someone led him to the attic, same someone *threw* him out of the window, probably hoped he'd be killed when he hit the ground, but it happened a different way. It remains murder – *three* murders, now!'

'It's pure guessing!' exclaimed Robin.

'Guessing?' repeated Folly in the awful voice of authority mocked, *'Guessing?* Three murders – but this is the last. Someone admitted Dering to this house tonight, got him into the attic. Probably knocked him unconscious, perhaps killed him, first, then pushed him out of the window. He's a little

fellow – anyone here could have done it. Man or woman. I know who did it, too!'

'Who?' Robin asked, in a strangled voice.

'The same person who tipped Dering off about the necklace being under the shrubbery. Same person who killed Mottram, and tried to get us to suspect your wife. Someone who knew all about the family feud and the old theft – oh, a member of the family all right! I thought once that it was Battley, but he's safely in jail. Good thing for him.' Folly drew a deep breath, rising dramatically on his small, shining toes. 'It is someone now in this house! They had a means of communicating with Dering, made an appointment with him here, for tonight. Doubtless used the hassock for communicating. Got him here, told him what window to come to – ivy's easy to climb. We'll find the room he entered as soon as it's light. The criminal fixed everything perfectly – or thought so! The cut canvas, Dering's dead body, all the evidence of guilt – bah! He bungled it. If those pictures had been taken upstairs and cut out there, it *might* have succeeded, but Dering certainly didn't take them from the sitting-room and then walk up to the top of the house with them.'

He stopped, and stared broodingly at Dering's body. 'Someone wanted those pictures very badly. Silas Mottram had a number, all very similar – that's obvious enough. Only one of them seems valuable. By a process of elimination, we'll find which one. *The murderer acted to get those pictures.* Who was in the passage when you first appeared, Fayne?'

'My brother, and Lynda,' said Robin, slowly. 'William was upstairs. The door was broken, there is no doubt William broke it down. That was the noise that woke me up.'

'Wait a moment! Doesn't your brother know something about pictures?'

'Yes,' said Robin. 'Quite a bit.'

Folly led the way to the sitting-room.

The atmosphere, already brittle, seemed ready to splinter at a touch as he held out the rolls of canvas to Charles.

'There's something phoney about these. What is it?'

Charles, startled, took the pictures and looked at them one at a time. He stared at the poorly-executed portraits, one of Silas Mottram and the other – as Valerie now knew, of Dering, and began to pick, very delicately, at the canvas.

Folly said in a soft, deadly monotone:

'Who was against consulting the police? You were, Mottram. Got the evidence of your conversation. Others were, too, but you were most emphatic.'

'I object!' cried William. 'I –'

'You can object when I've finished. You were against it all the time. You wanted to hush everything up. You were insistent that it was Dering. My men have ears and they heard a lot. You tried to convince them that it was Dering. Ye-es. You were in the attic. Easy to have thrown Dering out, and then pretended to break down the door. *Very* easy. Thing is – why?'

William said, thickly:

'This is the most outrageous accusation! You have not heard the last of it. Percy! I instruct –'

'Not right now,' said Folly. 'Only I will do the instructing.' His glance, calm but intimidating, fell like a knife on Feldmann. 'Must be a reason,' went on Folly. 'A very strong reason.' He looked at Charles. 'Any result? No? Who *owns* those pictures?'

Feldmann said: 'All Silas Mottram's pictures were left to his nephew, Charles.'

'They were, were they? Commander, can you clean the pictures down? I want to see what's underneath? I suspect –'

'Oh, no,' said Charles, 'the canvas isn't old enough to be a disguised masterpiece. Some of the others that were at Crow's shop might have been painted over, but these are on new canvas. Uncle Silas's own work, too – I can guarantee that. No one else on earth would have used that red for the complexion!'

'Will you clean it down?' snapped Folly. 'They're your pictures, you've every right to. Have you got the material for the work?'

'I think there's some in the attic,' said Charles.

'I protest!' cried William. 'The pictures should not be touched. The will has not yet been proved, and it might not be upheld. The pictures then, would not belong to Charles!'

'That is so,' admitted Feldmann.

Robin said: 'Clean the picture, Charles, let's be done with it.'

William's shock was very evident. Suddenly, horrifyingly, age came to him and he appeared to sag. Charles eyed him with a look of incredulity, Lynda evenly, and Robin in obstinate disbelief. Charles, escorted by Webb, went upstairs for the cleaning materials and solvents. Once back he began to clean the varnish with skilful precision.

William stared, as if hypnotised by the sound of Charles's rubbing. The gentle monotony of sound ceased suddenly, as Charles looked up with blazing eyes.

'There *is* something here! Some paper, beneath the priming!'

He continued excitedly, 'Safest hiding place in the world. Here it comes! Heavy printing on the other side – it's face downwards, so the writing will be quite legible. Looks like a legal document.'

William put his hand to his pocket. He was trembling and his fingers were unsteady. Folly was staring at Charles, but Webb looked up and saw the barrister putting something to his mouth. Webb shouted, and leapt across the room, knocking William's hand aside. A small, white pellet dropped from his fingers, and was crushed beneath Webb's foot.

William had lost every vestige of colour as he stared at Webb, his lips working, then he dropped into a chair, his face in his hands. Lynda stepped towards him, and Charles, who had stopped rubbing, stared at them both. It was an odd, touching little scene. Lynda put a hand on William's shoulder, pressed gently and said:

'Hard luck, William! We did try, didn't we? But the last will and testament beat us.'

Chapter 28

Confession

William did not speak or move. Feldmann stepped forward, but Folly was the first to speak, his voice surprised, even chagrined.

'Both of you!' he exclaimed. *'Both!'*

Lynda began: 'We were –'

'Lynda, I advise you most strongly not to make any statement whatever,' said Feldmann, crisply. 'Anything you wish to say may be passed on through me, I will act for you. Folly, I am acting for her and William, who is overwrought, and I insist upon –'

Lynda's lips twisted, wryly.

'It's no use,' she said. 'Look at William!'

Feldmann reached her side.

'Don't go on,' he said, earnestly. 'Be advised by me, Lynda. You will do no one any good.'

'I'll do no one any harm,' said Lynda. 'We stood or fell by that will. It cuts both William and me out, completely. That wouldn't matter, only – it says why. He made it when he discovered that William and I dealt in faked and stolen pictures. That was some time ago, when we made our first and fatal mistake. We sold a fake to Uncle Silas.'

No one spoke.

'Silas discovered it,' went on Lynda. 'Instead of reporting it, or warning us off, he let us sweat in fear that he would one day make the disclosure. And he kept dropping hints. He made *his* mistake when he told us that he'd cut us out of the will and had given his reasons, quoting chapter and verse. He'd got the whole case proved. He told us he knew that it would make us more anxious than ever to kill him, but that if we did so, he would have his revenge from the grave. Neither of us had thought of killing him before that. We decided then that we'd have to find and destroy the will, and afterwards kill him.

'Dering told us how the will was hidden,' she continued. 'Apparently he saw it being done, but he wasn't sure which picture was used. He was one of the men who introduced us to fakes. Dering promised that if we killed Silas he would get hold of all the pictures and destroy the will.'

'Why did Dering want Silas killed?' asked Folly.

'He had been selling Silas fakes for some time,' said Lynda, 'and Silas was on the point of denouncing him. Dering rented The Paddocks after William and I started to work with him, you see. He saw a chance of blackmailing the whole family, but Silas's unconcern for his relatives made that impossible. Dering was a thorough-going rogue. He was a fence – yes, he even used the church for a temporary hiding-place! He thought he would be quite safe if we killed Silas, he intended to confuse the trails, and, goodness knows, he tried! Then Silas started his campaign against Dering – he asked for police protection because of Dering, who became difficult – by making him leave The Paddocks. Dering himself was working up to something much bigger. Then Silas wondered if *we* were in the plot to murder him, after all, so he called the conference. Dering – who stole the necklace back from Silas – managed to stop the conference.

'Silas was getting badly worried by then,' went on Lynda, 'and he'd pretty well decided to go to the police about it all. We knew we had a soft spot for Charles, so we faked a message from Charles and got him to visit the house on Monday night. We were waiting for him at the end of the drive. We overpowered him and carried him to the garage, where we killed him.' She drew a deep breath. 'It was – ' her face was very pale – 'it was ridiculously easy. The man who had tormented us for years was dead, and could do us no more harm. I didn't think of the consequences. I had some vague idea of carrying him away somewhere, but – we reckoned without Dering.'

She stopped. When she spoke again it was with a great effort, and the words came slowly.

'Yes, we reckoned without Dering. We knew that he was a rogue, but we were fools enough to think that he would keep his promise. Instead, he arrived soon afterwards, with his man, Chesterton. He told us to get away, and promised to look after the body. We couldn't make any conditions. We didn't think, then, that he was going to double-cross us. We trusted him, not knowing that he arranged it all so that Valerie and Robin would be the chief suspects. He believed the police would work until they found someone. It was he who stole the canvases which started you thinking about them. He was looking for the one which had Silas's will, for he knew that would damn us, and he was after us for lifelong blackmail. He missed it, so he started all manner of red-herrings – the leaving of the diamonds, for instance, taking them away again, putting saw-dust in the attic, even putting drops of blood from a dead rabbit on the attic floor.'

Webb rubbed his chin, slowly.

'We didn't see him, after Monday night,' said Lynda, 'but we picked up a message – he told us he was coming here tonight, and we must find a way of letting him in. I sent a message back. You see, we had to get those pictures out of the house, and we couldn't take them ourselves for fear of being caught with them. We had to trust Dering, even then! William cut the canvases out of the frames, when everyone had gone to bed.

'Then Dering arrived.

'William gave him the canvases, then told him to stop implicating other members of the family. Dering just laughed at him. He said that we were in no position to make conditions, he could have us denounced both for the murder and for our earlier associations with him. William argued, and then – ' she drew a deep breath. 'Then Dering told us that he had built up a second identity – in London. He was going to disappear, and would deal with us only through third parties. And he said that Robin and Charles would probably be hanged for Crow's murder. William accused him of that, and he admitted it. Oh, he felt quite safe! Apparently Silas had consulted Crow about the fakes, and Crow was going to examine them.'

For the first time, Folly interrupted.

'When did Crow start work on the pictures?'

'I can only tell you what Dering told us,' said Lynda. 'After you and Inspector Webb had left the shop, Crow set to work immediately, but Dering was watching the shop. Apparently, Crow assumed that Dering had murdered Silas, because Silas was on the point of discovering that he had sold him fakes. Dering dared not allow him to inform the police – '

'Would Crow have done that?' asked Folly.

Lynda paused, and lit a cigarette. Her fingers trembled, the cigarette shook between her lips, and she did not go on until she had recovered enough to speak steadily. Most of the time, she looked at William's bowed head.

'Yes, he would have done so, he was as honest as they come,' she said, at last. 'Poor little Crow! William was more angry about his murder than anything else, but Dering laughed in our faces. He had worked so cunningly and tortuously, that he believed he had pulled it off. He thought he could get away with the murder he had done, that he would be able to victimise us, and that we would even stand by and see our own relations hanged. You should have seen William then,' she added, softly. 'He was perfect! He didn't raise his voice, but declared he was done with it and would summon the police, who were already on the premises, and make a full confession. When Dering realised that he was serious, he drew a knife. I think he meant to frighten us. I threw a book at him, and William hit him as he dodged. I think the blow broke his neck – anyhow, he was unconscious. We decided to drop him out of the window, and hope that it would look as though he had broken in, stolen the pictures, and fallen while climbing out of the window. It seemed the perfect solution, and we filled his pockets with all the oddments which would draw suspicion on him. Just for a few seconds, we thought it might settle everything. Dering would be presumed guilty of the first two crimes, and while the latter will remain hidden, there was nothing against us except that we couldn't account for our movements on Monday night.' She looked into Folly's eyes, and added: 'We might have succeeded if you hadn't been so sure about the pictures being cut out down here.'

After a tense silence, Folly said:

'Ye-es, possibly. Miss Mottram, why did your brother William talk so convincingly of Dering as the murderer?'

Lynda said: 'Dering always boasted that he could disappear completely, as I've said, although we didn't know that he had created another identity for himself in London, and that as Dering he was going to disappear. Even Chesterton did not know what his new identity was going to be.'

Folly's eyes widened. 'Well, well!' he exclaimed. 'No wonder Chesterton talked so freely about his Guv'nor!'

'All Dering and Chesterton were doing was putting the

whole affair into confusion,' said Lynda. 'Chesterton hated Battley, too. Dering even boasted tonight that Battley would also be framed. Chesterton had been to his cottage, pretending to look for pictures, but actually to leave something incriminating. You fell for that when you arrested Battley.'

'Not quite,' said Folly. 'Not quite, Miss Mottram. It is now my duty to – '

Lynda said: 'Never mind that. I know what's going to happen, but – ' she looked towards Valerie, her eyes appealing. 'Val,' she said, and paused. 'Val, it was Dering who was trying to implicate you – not William or I. You will believe that?'

William and Lynda were taken into Listow. The macabre tidying up, the last dismal processes of the law set in motion, Folly and Webb left The Paddocks.

'Satisfied Webb?' asked Folly, and then: 'Of course you are! Pity the girl was in it, but – well, she knew the stakes she was playing for as clearly as Mottram, probably.'

'Ye-es,' said Webb. 'I suppose I'm satisfied. I certainly know my job better than I did! You were – '

'Hush!' exclaimed Folly. 'Just a trick, that's all. Taking it by and large, its been a beauty of a case – haven't come across a better. One curious thing – how Feldmann changed when he began to realise that Silas was an evil genius. Oh, yes, Silas was a very nasty piece of work.'

'Not worth dying for,' said Webb.

'A dangerous doctrine,' said Folly soberly, 'that once beckoned a German monomaniac, and could do again. Safer to stick to a life for a life. Still, a good barrister will probably make the jury agree with you, and recommend them to mercy on the grounds of extreme provocation. He'll play up to the strong provocation for attacking Dering, too, and probably get the charge reduced to manslaughter. If old Crow hadn't kept his ideas to himself until he had proof that Dering dealt in fakes, we might have stopped a lot. *Might* have.'